Praise for *Crazy Love*

"Leslie What finds a surreal joy in the most awful things that can happen."
 —Eileen Gunn, author of *Stable Strategies and Others*

"At times deeply emotional and mature but also clever and entertaining, Leslie What's short fiction always comes from the heart. A collection from her can only be a cause for celebration."
 —Jeff VanderMeer, author of *Shriek, an Afterward*

"Classic Leslie What."
 —Bill Sullivan, author of *Listening for Coyote: A Walk Across Oregon's Wilderness*

Praise of *Olympic Games*, Tachyon, 2004

"Take a playboy Zeus with issues; a New-Age Hera; an idiot boy; another who's half-bug, half-bat; an artist who walks backwards; and a woman who lived inside a door for 2000 years... You'd think with this melange, no one but Eudora Welty could have made a moving and magical novel. You'd be wrong. Leslie What has."
 —Howard Waldrop

"*Olympic Games* is not only the first novel by one of our most gifted fantasists, it's a revelation.'"
 —James Patrick Kelly

"If anybody can write about gods and goddesses, it's Leslie What. She's had more close encounters with them than anybody else I know. In fact, I suspect she's actually a goddess-in-hiding. Read on for a tantalizing and tasty serving of divine madness."
 —Nina Kiriki Hoffman

"The Queen of Gonzo."
 —Gardner Dozois, editor of *Isaac Asimov's*

"This novel is so much fun. From the woman in the door to bug bangs (not the haircut) and beyond, the story is deeply imagined and wonderfully realized. Yes, the book is a romp with the gods being the gods, but it is also full of people you will come to care about like Penelope, and Possum who is used to moody women, and Eddie who is destined for bigger things—people who will linger in your mind long after you've turned the last page."
—Ray Vukcevich

"...a great big scary comic talent."
—Damon Knight

"This is a wonderful novel; it may well become a cult classic."
—Elizabeth Hand

"This very funny fantasy is especially impressive in the way it turns serious and genuinely moving in its final pages."
—Michael Berry, *San Fransisco Chronicle*

Praise for *The Sweet and Sour Tongue*, Wildside, 2002

"Her ingenious whimsey takes her tales to a whole other level of sublime metaphor and surreality."
—*Publisher's Weekly*

Crazy Love

ISBN: 978-1-877655-59-3
Library of Congress Number: 2008921844

Publication Date: July 2008

Cover Art, "Wallpaper", Jessica Plattner
(www.jessicaplattner.com)
Cover Design: Kristin Summers
(www.redbatdesign.com)
Text Design by David Memmott
Author photo by What Lunch Enterprises

Published by
Wordcraft of Oregon, LLC
P.O. Box 3235
La Grande, OR 97850

editor@wordcraftoforegon.com

Member of Council of Literary Magazines & Presses (CLMP),
PMA, The Independent Book Publishers Association
& The Speculative Literature Foundation Small Press Co-op

Printed in the United States of America

CRAZY LOVE
STORIES By LESLIE WHAT

2008

for Gary

Leslie and Gary sitting in a tree
K-I-S-S-I-N-G
First comes love
Then comes marriage
Then comes Junior in a baby carriage

—Jump rope rhyme

TABLE OF CONTENTS

Introduction by Kate Wilhelm 11
Finger Talk 13
Babies.. 30
The Cost of Doing Business... 44
Frankenfetish 56
All My Children 66
I Remember Marta 82
Love Me 93
The Mutable Borders Of Love 97
Paper Mates 110
Picture a World Where All Men Are Named Harry 116
Storytime 121
That Jellyfish Man Keeps A-Rolling.. 129
The Changeling 141
The Wereslut of Avenue A... 148
Going Vampire 156
Why a Duck... 168
My Hermit... 179

iNTRODUCTiON

"Love is a many splendored thing."
"Love makes the world go round."
"All it takes is love."

The stories you'll find in this slim volume wouldn't fit into any of the above, nor would they ever be found in the old true romance magazines. Sometimes satirical, sometimes wickedly funny, cruel, compassionate, over the top—whatever description one chooses to use, it very likely will apply to a story here. They all share some qualities such as closely observed, honestly related, beautifully crafted, and always deeply meaningful to the characters involved. There is frequently startling poignancy as the stories twist and turn in unexpected ways. These are real love stories—love found, love lost, love sought, love bought, love betrayed . . .

Another cliché: The path of true love never runs smooth. Very, very true.

Among the characters you'll meet in these pages:

The Jellyfish man, who resembles a jellyfish more than anything human and behaves as a sentient street cleaner. Repugnant, hideous, nursing a long time grievance, suddenly he becomes a person to pity, yearning, yearning.

A lesbian desperately afraid of losing her lover, who happens to be a werewolf.

The father of ten thousand, who has lost the only two children who are important to him.

A woman who loves and is protective of a multitude of embryos developing in her womb. Or is it a swarm?

A young woman who works in a gorilla suit and receives a life-changing message from Coco the talking gorilla by way of television.

A woman who decides she would prefer to be a victim rather than continue as a loser.

Ghosts who lost the battle of love, which always includes winners and losers, and in which the price of losing is your life.

A vampire who is a Hollywood agent and ponders if it is possible for such as he to fall in love.

These are not your typical suburban characters engaged in the endless suburban courtship rituals, the marital squabbles, the extramarital affairs, nor are they the sophisticated Sex in the City set with casual affairs in the making or the breaking. These characters, sometimes dark and perverse, outre, other-worldly, are beautifully realized, and are true to the situations they find themselves in. Their problems are real, their pain real. We must accept finally, with whatever degree of reluctance we arrive at the conclusion, that they also represent an aspect of the human condition common to all of us, regardless of how deeply buried and never acknowledged each of us has managed to keep that aspect.

The stories should not be read in a single sitting. Although the volume is slim, the stories are not. They are weighty, powerful, strong medicine, too strong to be taken all at once.

Kate Wilhelm
January 10, 2008

FiNGER TALK

First appeared in *Mota: Truth*,
Tripletree Publishing, 2003

Koko, the talking gorilla, was on the television again the
August afternoon I went to Tom's place to convince him
to love me. Seemed I'd seen Koko on television pretty often.
Seemed I'd been at Tom's place more than usual, too. Tom had
never been to my place; it was that type of relationship.

I sat on the couch next to Tom and took off my gorilla head
in order to see his television a little better. I had raced to get there
after work, and was still inside my fake-fur gorilla suit uniform,
so I was really hot and sweaty. My job was delivering candy and
flower baskets to people's homes and offices. I was my own boss
and my only employee. I called myself the *Independence Day
Gorilla*, though I would soon become the *Labor Day Gorilla*,
and a couple of months after that, would change into my winter
name—the *Santa Gorilla*. In Spring I'd become the *Easter Gorilla*
and from there, the cycle repeated. This was my first four-season
job, which meant that I was broke all year round. To make extra
money on the side, I worked as a minister in my own church,
presiding over weddings and funerals. Unfortunately, it had been
a slow season for human gorillas and ministers, and I already
owed rent for September, even though I hadn't paid since June.

I felt interested in Koko for reasons I didn't understand.
Maybe because she was the only person I knew who was born
Goth. The rest of us painted our nails dark and wore all-black

outfits to get Koko's look. Or maybe it was because we had so much in common, like being formerly homeless, and hating alligators, and losing our babies—even though, technically, for her it had been a kitten and not even her baby, and I hadn't lost mine yet. Koko and that lady scientist who acted like her mother were coming to Southern California to raise the money for a wildlife preserve for talking gorillas.

Right there on the news, Koko moved her fingers and that lady scientist translated it as saying, "I miss my baby." It had been a long time, but Koko was still grieving over a kitten she had loved who had died when Koko was a little girl gorilla. The lady scientist stroked Koko's hairy arm and told the newsman that finger talk proved gorillas were intelligent.

Unlike Koko, I did not want a baby and I wished like anything our *situations* were reversed, and that I could have a lady scientist to take care of me, and that Koko could have my baby. I wished I could talk to Koko and ask her advice. I wanted to know how she stayed fresh in summer in a solar-collector fur coat, because I was sweating like a George Bush trying to explain the war in Iraq. I wanted to show Koko how I'd re-painted my whole life, including my one-room studio apartment, all black, to match my clothes. I wanted to ask her if she was happier living with the lady scientist than when she was homeless in the jungle. I wanted to ask her why I wasn't happy, even though I had a house and a car and a boyfriend, everything I always thought I wanted.

I inherited five-thousand dollars when my mother died, and I used the money to buy a sewing machine and black fake fur and a car: a 1964 black Cadillac Coupe De Ville convertible, from a man named Elvis, the only Elvis who became famous for not being famous, even though his name was Elvis. His car lot was called Unfamous Elvis Cars and he advertised on late night TV, which was how I found him. He told me he was giving me a good deal, and if I fixed up the upholstery and redid the engine, I could sell it for twice as much as I had paid for it. Maybe that was true, but I spent the last of my money on the car and didn't have any left over for the engine. In fact, I'd spent so much money on the car, I didn't have any left over to deal with my *situation*.

I had only a few days before the day I had to decide if I was going to "expel the contents of the uterus," as the hairy-legged lady at the feminist women's clinic had called it, or carry "the products of conception" to term.

I snuck a look Tom's way and felt so lucky to have him as my boyfriend. Tom had dark skin the color of a well-done tan, dark eyes, dark hair, and a dark mustache that covered the top half of his lip. Tom was really cute and I was wildly in love with him, so in love, that I was blind as to how to break the news about my *situation*.

Koko had been in the news so much that it was plain to see how much that lady scientist loved her. But not everybody shared that kind of love, and some religious nuts were protesting her visit because they thought that talking gorillas were against God. If Koko had learned English instead of sign language, there wouldn't have been so much controversy. As it was, everyone in Southern California had different ideas about what Koko was trying to say. Some said she was only parroting the lady scientist, but I strongly disagreed. Not that I knew much sign language, having only learned the alphabet watching Sesame Street. Koko knew at least 2000 words.

Tom reached over and tried to pull down the zipper at the back of my suit. The teeth had somehow gotten jammed up with fake-fur and Tom was having a heck of a time undoing that zipper. He didn't say anything about the fact that I was wearing the bottom three-quarters of a fake-fur gorilla suit, except, "Damn that zipper, Delilah!" Finally, he gave up and reached for his beer bottle from the metal keg he'd had reincarnated into a table. To tell you the truth, that was fine with me. Because of my present *situation*, I can tell you I was really not in the mood.

"What ya think about Koko?" I asked.

"Who the fuck is Koko?" Tom said.

"You know. The talking gorilla," I said.

15

"Gorillas can't talk," Tom said.

Well I didn't have much to say after that, either. Only I did, I just didn't know how to say it. I had to tell Tom about "the contents of my uterus." I had to find out about Tom's plans so I could make my plans. Thing was, I was scared Tom would break up with me once he learned my *situation*. Worse, I was scared Tom couldn't care less what my *situation* was.

"Why don't you go home," Tom said, so I did.

Tom's place was at the bottom back of a four-plex. I let myself out and ran along the walkway to the street. My Cadillac was parked out front, just like always. I drove the ten blocks to my place. My landlady was pulling weeds in a constipated flower garden the size of a chest x-ray and saw me pull up. She smiled and said, "Everything okay?" She had always been so kind to me and I loved her like a sister. But I couldn't tell her anything about my *situation*, because she couldn't have any babies, even though she wanted to, and I was afraid she might try to get me to have one for her.

I went inside to watch what was left of the news. My apartment was a dark room above a garage I didn't even get to park in. The landlady got to park in it, and she and her husband owned Buicks, in my opinion, not cars worth protecting from the elements. They also owned electric garage door openers and sometimes I could hear the door go up and down when they were coming or going.

There were only two little windows so my studio stayed really hot. On TV, the weatherman said that this particular August heat wave was the hottest one on record. I couldn't help but wonder how Koko was handling things, because it felt really hot inside my gorilla suit. Maybe she was more used to the heat and all, since she lived in Hawaii, or maybe she made enough money to pay for air-conditioning. I'd have done just about anything to get air-conditioning myself, it was that hot, even with the windows open.

Things improved a little once I finally wriggled out of my gorilla suit, but I was still stuck with worry about how I was gonna get the money to take care of my *situation*.

By Sunday morning I'd decided on a plan. When I first got my sewing machine and black fake fur, I had sewn some extra gorilla suits, just in case, and now I packed three of them inside the old alligator suitcase I'd inherited from my mother. I kept out the fourth to wear for a demonstration unit and I wore it and drove out to the Sunday swap meet. This was Los Angeles, California, which explains why I had a car even though I didn't have much money and had to choose between gasoline and food. Everybody drove there. Everybody, probably even Koko had her own learner's permit.

My Cadillac had 100,000 miles on it and the convertible top didn't work so good, so I had to be careful not to take it out in the rain. It was not raining that Sunday and there wasn't a spot of shade anywhere at the swap meet, which was really a re-incarnated drive-in theater. Most everyone who sold at the swap meet brought shade umbrellas, but I hadn't even thought of that until it was too late. I spent all morning sitting on top of my old alligator suitcase, sweating in my solar-collector black gorilla suit.

"You poor dear," this lonely little old lady next-door at a table in what used to be a parking space said. "You must be so hot." She'd set up her blue umbrella to cast a shadow over her lawn chair to stay cool.

"Well, I am warm," I said. I wasn't sure if she understood me because the fake-fur muffled my words.

This lonely little old lady sold really cute walnut shell mouses. She made them with half a walnut shell, onto which she'd glued those plastic eyes with the floating black dots in the middle, and leather ears in the front. Then she glued leather tails on the backs of the walnut shell. She was selling a lot of walnut shell mouses.

You'd have thought everyone in California had been waiting for that particular Sunday to come to the Sunday swap meet so they could buy walnut shell mouses. Whereas nobody had been waiting for that particular Sunday to get their gorilla suits. So I marked everything down half price, hoping that would help.

"I don't seem to have many customers," I said, pulling apart the fake-fur mouth, lion-tamer style, so she could hear me.

"Don't worry," said the old lady. "It takes a few weeks before people realize you're here."

"Thanks," I said, but I did not understand how people could pass someone dressed in a gorilla suit without seeing she was there. Besides, I didn't have a few weeks. I had one, two at most. If it wasn't for those cute little walnut shell mice to cheer me up, I would have cried.

That Sunday I sold gorilla suits at the Sunday swap meet, not a single person bought one. In the afternoon one child brought her mother over to look at how cute the child looked in a gorilla mask. The child's mother gave me a dollar and said, "Thanks."

I bought one of the old lady's walnut shell mouses with my dollar. She told me that she donated all her profits to charity. I really liked her. She could have been a saint, except she wasn't famous enough to have anyone make towels out of her likeness.

At five o'clock I drove home, pretty disappointed. I took off my gorilla suit and took a shower and changed into the only summer dress that still fit over my belly. I called Tom and he wasn't home, so I switched on the TV and saw Koko on the news again. A guy interviewed Koko and that lady scientist. Koko's fingers moved like she was telling the newsman she wasn't bullshitting him. The guy didn't understand finger talk, so he didn't really know if Koko was talking or just wiggling, but he argued with that lady anyway. This wasn't a call-in show or I might have called him to tell the guy I thought Koko had said something. Instead, I dialed my Tom's number and this time he was home.

"Hi," I said. "It's Delilah." I told Tom my name because, even though we had been going together since June and I was pregnant by him, he never seemed to recognize my voice.

"Yeah. Hi," Tom said. He took a long chug of something. "I was waiting for you to call," Tom said.

"What are you doing tonight?" I asked.

"Drinking beer, picking up a girl unless you come over," Tom said.

"Do you want to come over here?" I asked.

"Hell, Delilah," Tom said. "It's too damn hot to move, and I don't even know where you live."

"Should I come over there?" I asked.

"Just get here before I go out," Tom said.

Now I know everyone reading this is thinking: why did she put up with this guy? Because I was thinking it too. The thing was, by the time I was thinking about not putting up with Tom, I was already in my *situation*. I had already put up with Tom long enough that not putting up with him would have been anti-climactic.

"Don't go until I get there," I said. I wanted to ask him what he planned to do so that I could decide what I planned to do. I drove to Tom's place, fast, because even though Tom lived close, I was afraid he might leave before I got there. I parked my car on the street and walked around to his door.

He opened the door on the seventh ring.

"What took you so long?" he asked.

His attitude didn't bother me much, though it's easy to look back on it now and see I was a little off in my judgment. Some of that might have been due to hormones and not my fault.

"You're so funny," I said. I shook my head like I was in on his little joke.

He invited me in. He wore one of those low-cut undershirts under a black leather jacket. He was so cute. I could not believe he was my boyfriend.

"Well what are we doing tonight?" I asked Tom.

"You driving?" he said.

"Sure," I said.

"Then let's go to the beach," Tom said.

He put his arm around me and we walked to my car. He jumped over the door to get to his seat instead of opening the door. I think that was one reason why he liked me, because I had a Cadillac. I'd known when I bought my car that a black Cadillac was the ticket to love.

I headed toward the freeway. Tom turned on the radio and we both started singing a Beach Boy song. That was fun. Then there was a news flash, and I heard that lady scientist telling people to come to the civic auditorium the next night and see Koko up close.

"What do you think about Koko?" I asked Tom.

"Who the fuck is Koko?" Tom said back.

"You know. The one we watched on TV," I said. "The talking gorilla."

"Gorillas can't talk," Tom said.

Wasn't much to say after that.

We drove to the beach and I parked in a public lot. We got out of the car to walk along the sand, and we took off our sandals and got our feet wet in the ocean.

"See any grunion tonight?" Tom asked and I stopped walking to look. He started to pull me down on the sand, but I had done that with him once before, and let me tell you, without a blanket or some other form of protection, sex in the sand is not romantic.

"Do I look like a crab?" I said.

When we did it in the sand the last time, I turned into an egg timer. There was sand in my mouth, sand in my eyes, sand in my ears and in between my fingers and toes. I had to stand on my head to get the sand outside of my insides. That August sixteenth night when Tom wanted to do it in the sand, I took him back to the car and let him do it in the back seat of the Cadillac. My mind was elsewhere, or I would have been doing it too.

"I love you, Delilah," Tom said while he was doing it. And God help me I believed him. I believed Tom because I loved him more than anything. Well to get on with it. I drove Tom home. I was about to tell him about the contents of my uterus. "Tom," I was going to say. "Remember how you took the twenty dollars I needed to pick up my birth control prescription and you bought beer?"

I had almost got my nerve to speak when Tom asked if he could drop me off at my place. Tom said he wanted to borrow my car, and he'd pick me up later, and then we could be together.

"I'll come back to spend the night with you," Tom said, and I wanted to believe him.

When Tom didn't come back that night, or even in the morning I knew I had some deciding to do. Not that there was much of a choice. It was now August seventeenth and I needed money to get an abortion.

The only things of value that I owned those days, besides my car, my alligator suitcase, and my couch, were those handmade gorilla suits, plus that walnut shell mouse. Well, I was not about to sell that cute little mouse. So, I got this idea to go door-to-door and sell gorilla suits. The way I figured it, I was exactly four gorilla suits short of an abortion. I put on my regular gorilla suit for demonstration and started up the street with the three others in my suitcase. I held the walnut shell mouse in one free hand for good luck.

I had lived in that neighborhood since May, but besides my landlady, I didn't know any of the neighbors by name. Even if I did, they wouldn't have recognized me underneath my gorilla suit. I walked up to each house, rang the doorbell, and when somebody answered the door, I started my routine.

"Hello," I said. "I'm selling gorilla suits to work my way through college." I told that lie because I wasn't about to tell anyone about my personal troubles. Well I'm sure that by now they've done studies and everything to find out what the best way to sell gorilla suits door-to-door, but back then, I was on my own.

I went up to a little brick house and who should open the

door but the lonely little old lady! Of course she remembered me and invited me inside for some ice tea. I could tell she lived by herself and never had anyone to talk to because she was anxious to talk to me. She had her television turned on extremely loud, and you-know-who was in the news again.

"Make yourself comfortable," said the old lady.

I took off my mask to drink my tea and put my little walnut shell mouse on her coffee table.

"I just love your little mouse," I yelled, and she said, "Thank you so much!" like she really meant it.

Koko's fingers were wiggling and moving every way to tell the newsman that she was not trying to bullshit him. Even I could tell that, and I only knew the sign language alphabet.

All of a sudden, that lady scientist turned angry. "What is the matter with you?" she cried out. "Can't you see there's other intelligent life on this planet?" Something about what she said really got to me, and I started bawling right there on the old lady's couch because I knew there was other intelligent life on this planet.

When the old lady invited me into her house, I am sure she had no idea I was going to go crazy on her couch. The only decent thing to do was stand up and make ready to leave. The old lady, bless her heart, looked at me and told me to sit back down. She pointed to my walnut shell mouse.

"Did you ever think about making that mouse into a refrigerator magnet?" she asked.

I shrugged my shoulders and she said, "I have some extra magnets and a bottle of glue. Why don't you keep yourself busy while I make you a little dinner? She brought me the supplies and left to microwave a tuna-pot-pie, because that was all she had in her freezer that wasn't already planned for a meal. I finished my refrigerator mouse magnet and put it on the coffee table to dry.

I had never had microwaved potpie, at least that I knew about. Microwaved tuna-pot-pie tasted strange because the crust was doughy, like it wasn't cooked, only it was. If I could have done things differently that day, I would have. There are so many things I would have changed, including that first big bite of tuna-pot-pie. The doughy potpie made me sick to my stomach, and before I could stop, I chucked all over my gorilla suit.

I broke down into tears again. The old lady brought me some paper towels to wipe off my gorilla suit and a wet washcloth to cool my face.

"What in the world is the matter?" she said, but in a sweet way, not like she thought I was an idiot. "What happened to you that forced you to sell gorilla suits door-to-door for a living?"

"I'm pregnant," I said. I blurted it out, just like that. Besides the hairy-legged lady at the feminist women's clinic who had pressed really hard on my stomach like she had to prove she was as strong as a man, no one else knew. I didn't know why, but the old lady understood exactly why my being pregnant explained the gorilla suit business. She took out her wallet and bought me out of gorilla suits. If I hadn't chucked over that demonstration suit, she'd have bought that one too.

"What do you plan to do with those gorilla suits?"

"I've got a son in Oregon," she said, like that explained it.

I still needed twenty more dollars or else I was gonna end up with a baby. The old lady wrote down her address and phone number and told me to call her if I needed anything else. She really meant it, but I was too embarrassed to ask for any more money. I went into the bathroom and splashed some water on my face. I couldn't help but notice that I was starting to smell pretty ripe. The zipper was stuck fast and there was no way to get inside my suit to freshen up any better, so I gargled with the old lady's mouthwash, then dribbled a little inside of the fake-fur neck. The minty odor wafted up and sort of cleared out some of the muddy feelings in my head. I made a decision to go see Koko's lecture.

I grabbed my gorilla head and my walnut shell mouse, which was now a magnet, and walked outside to the intersection. I rolled my gorilla mask into a ball and held it under my arm. It was really hot outside and I looked like shit, smelled worse. I'd have given anything to take off my suit and just wear the shorts and tee shirt I had on underneath, but I didn't dare mess with anything until later, when I could take my time to work the zipper open. I didn't know what I'd do the next time I had to go to the bathroom. This was not an ideal *situation* in more ways than one.

Still, the second I stuck out my thumb to hitchhike, some guy picked me up. That was one nice thing about being a girl.

"Where are you headed?" asked the guy.

Not that there was any choice. If there was anyone I wanted to talk to, it was Koko. I felt like we had an understanding, or something. "Civic Auditorium," I said.

"What's there?" he asked.

"Koko, the talking gorilla," I said.

"Oh," this guy said, like that explained *everything*. Neither one of us talked for the next twenty minutes. He dropped me off at the back of a line waiting to see Koko. The entrance was mobbed and a group of us latecomers were herded inside to the back. I was pushed into a line of people to stand in the center aisle in back of the back row of chairs. A kid in front of me turned and saw me holding a gorilla head. "Can I put it on?" he asked, but his mother slapped his hand and told him no.

There must have been two hundred people in that little auditorium; the place was completely packed. This prim lady who stood next door to me was wearing one of those khaki jump suits zipped from crotch to neck. She wrinkled up her nose when she got wind of me, a look that reminded me I probably smelled like a gorilla in the wild. This prim lady clutched her zipper pull like she wasn't about to let go of it. I don't know what she thought I was gonna do, but this prim lady would have moved away, if she could have, I'm sure.

Then the moderator introduced Koko and that lady scientist. There was applause and lots of boos. I could hardly believe that I was right there with them. That lady scientist's eyes were tired, but she smiled at Koko with the look of true love. I smiled too, seeing Koko in the flesh. I'd never seen a more beautiful creature. Silky fur, nothing like my matted up gorilla suit, clear eyes like the shiny part of night. If I wasn't so penned in at the back I would have rushed up to kiss her. Then the moderator introduced that lady scientist and Koko, the talking gorilla. Some people applauded and some booed. The lady's eyes looked kind of tired, but she smiled at Koko with the look of true love.

"I'd like to introduce you to Koko," said that lady scientist. "Say hello," she said to Koko.

Koko paused like she wanted to scratch her butt but didn't want to offend her mother. I knew that feeling well, which was how come I recognized it. Koko's fingers talked and that lady scientist translated.

"Hello," Koko/lady scientist said. "I am Koko." Koko might have said, "I'm Koko," only I wasn't sure if gorillas knew about contractions or not. I remembered contractions from grade school, but I didn't really know what kind of education gorillas got, so that's how come I wasn't exactly sure what she was saying.

Koko's fingers talked some more, but before that lady scientist had the chance to translate, this prim lady next door to me started screaming with the gift of tongues. Everyone turned around to stare at her. All her words were strung together in one gigantic sentence. You could understand the words one by one, but as a whole the prim lady made no sense, whatsoever. Security guards sort of paced along the aisle edges like they were trying to get closer to this prim lady, but couldn't get through.

"Mark-devil-six-fear-angel-god-beast," this prim lady said, only in gibberish and a lot longer than the above example.

"Glossolalia," said that lady scientist.

The whole time this was going on in the back of the auditorium, Koko stayed on the stage as calm as could be. I half-expected Koko to light up a cigarette.

Maybe because I was standing next to this prim lady; maybe because I was wearing the bottom three-quarters of a fake-fur gorilla suit; maybe for reasons that can only be described as cosmic, Koko looked at me like I was a kindred spirit, or something. I swear to God. Koko's fingers talked and that lady scientist put on glasses to look at who Koko was talking about. Everyone else thought Koko and that lady scientist were looking at this prim lady with the gift of tongues, but Koko and that lady scientist were not looking at her, they were looking at me.

"I understand you," said Koko/lady scientist.

"What's she saying?" asked the moderator, meaning, what's this prim lady saying?

"The lady should speak for herself," said Koko/lady scientist. I thought for a minute that maybe something got lost in that translation. I looked into Koko's eyes and I started to bawl because all at once it came to me, like in a vision. "Talk for yourself," was exactly what she'd said.

Her fingers began to fly and then a miracle happened. I suddenly understood every word Koko said. It was like I was Koko and Koko was me. Then Koko started to bawl and then that lady scientist started to bawl. And then I started to bawl even harder. The prim lady made the sign of the cross with her fingers and tried to back away.

Well this was just too much for me to take right then. I mean, Je-sus, this was Southern California. I had to get out of there. And the funny thing was, all these people who wouldn't move for the armed security guards took one whiff of me and let me pass.

Koko had told me in gorilla language that I had to tell Tom I was pregnant. I guess that's how gorillas handled similar *situations*. Gorillas mated for life and it was hard for Koko to understand things from my perspective. Humans, especially our men, can fuck without love.

I made my way to the street and thumbed a ride to my place. My car was not in front of my place so I walked to Tom's four-plex and saw my Cadillac on the street. I had never gone up to Tom's door without calling first, but by ten PM on August seventeenth, I had nothing left to lose.

I heard Tom yell from inside, "Get the door."

I'm not sure what the strange girl who answered the door

thought when she saw me on the other side of the threshold. She might have sensed something territorial was going on or else sensed something dangerous was about to happen, because she stepped aside to let me in, then ran away.

Tom lay on the couch with his pants part ways unzipped. His zipper was in his crotch, like all men's zippers and he'd been drinking. He started to raise his head like he was gonna get up, but he was so drunk, he just slumped back down.

"Je-sus Christ," Tom said, looking at me. "Delilah, I knew you was crazy."

"Crazy?" I said. I may have smelled like a gorilla in the wild, but I wasn't crazy. What I *was* was in love with someone who treated me like shit and was ignorant about my current *situation*. What I *was* was without any money for the abortion. What I *was* was depressed since I knew Tom didn't give a shit what I *was*.

Now what was I supposed to tell a man who treated me like shit when I knew he didn't give a shit what I said? I ended up handling it like this. My fingers were slow, because I didn't know sign language too good, but I spelled it out. "F-U-C-K Y-O-U," my fingers said. "A-S-S-H-O-L-E" they said, as an afterthought.

Trouble was, Tom didn't understand a word I said, but I felt good for having brought up the subject, anyway. Wasn't much left to say, after that. "Call me," I said. "We need to talk."

I grabbed my gorilla head and prepared to go home. The keys to my black Cadillac were on the table by the couch and Tom's pigskin billfold was underneath the keys, with a twenty-dollar-bill stuck part ways out of the billfold. The way things were all set up, my car keys looked like they were picking Andrew Jackson's nose.

I took my car keys, took the twenty-dollar-bill out of Tom's billfold, and took off in my black Cadillac. I drove to the feminist women's clinic parking lot where the hairy-legged lady worked. I got into the back seat to go to sleep. I stayed there all night, snuggled inside of my gorilla suit. Believe it or not, I was comfortable.

*

The hairy-legged lady was the first one to start work. She let me inside and helped me fill out the forms and then she carefully unzipped the back of my gorilla suit. She must have known from experience where the zipper was. She gave me two of those cotton gowns, and I put one on in front and the other on in back. The hairy-legged lady didn't say a word about my gorilla suit. I'll bet you she was used to seeing young girls being pregnant being crazy.

I won't tell about the abortion in this story. It was too disgusting. I will say this. The whole time they were doing the abortion, I wore my gorilla mask. The hairy-legged lady let me wear it, even though the man doctor said it was dangerous, because I might choke on my own barf. The hairy-legged lady could tell it was not any more dangerous to let me wear my gorilla mask during my abortion than to not let me wear it. Personally, the way that I was feeling, I agree that it was safer.

When it was all over, the hairy-legged lady gave me chocolate chip cookies and orange juice and blankets and let me lie down on her vinyl couch. I was so comfortable I never wanted to leave there. If they would have had a television at that clinic, I would have stayed the rest of my life, but I felt I should get back home. I wanted to watch the nightly news in case Koko was on. I'd know by looking in her eyes what she was thinking about my *situation*. If there was anyone I wanted to talk to in all of California, it was Koko. I felt like we had an understanding, or something.

I had to wear my gorilla suit home, but by then it didn't matter; I was used to how I smelled. I went upstairs and turned up the phone ringer to make sure I'd hear it when it rang. I had some free time before the news came on so I hung up my gorilla head on the coat rack and squirted a little oil up and down the zipper pull on my suit until it got going pretty easy. I took some aspirin to cover up the pain and freshened up with a spit bath.

After that, I sat on the couch to look over my mail. My subscription to the *National Geographic* had just come and sure enough, there was an article about you-know-who and her mother. I started to read, half-expecting after the day I'd had for Koko to talk to me through the magazine.

Of course nothing like that happened and I finally got tired of reading and turned the television on to wait for the news. I really wanted to talk to Koko.

Now in my heart of hearts I knew no gorilla, talking or not, could reach through television and talk to me. No gorilla could do that. Not even Koko. But what I knew was gonna happen and what I wanted to have happen were two separate things, and I knew that too. Just like knowing Tom wasn't gonna call didn't keep me from wanting Tom to call. Knowing doesn't prevent you from wanting, and how well I know that, now.

See, it was more likely for Koko to reach through television and talk to me than for Tom to call me on the telephone.

For Tom to call me would have been a miracle.

Tom was never gonna call me and I knew that.

Tom couldn't have called me.

Tom didn't care where the fuck I lived and what's more, the guy didn't even know my number.

BABIES

First appeared in *The Third Alternative*,
issue #34, 2003

Roni Sue stood before the sink, pushed away from the counter by her swollen belly. Her shoulders hurt from straining to reach forward and her lower back ached from the extra weight she carried, now over thirty pounds. On Sunday, the ladies at church had told her she looked "positively glowing." It didn't matter how many times they repeated this lie because she hated being pregnant, hated each and every hour. The best she could do was remind herself that soon she would be blessed with babies, lots of tiny babies, and the bad parts would all be over.

She wore the tricot slip she had bought at a yard sale, the only thing she owned still big enough and cool enough to sleep in. The slip had turned gray after being washed with Marc's jeans; the color and her huge belly made Roni Sue feel like an elephant. She would have thrown the slip away had the fabric not felt gossamer soft against her skin.

"Breakfast ready yet?" Marc called from the bathroom.

"Almost," she said.

A jellybean-sized cockroach hid in a crevice where the tile met the counter. A sliver of its membranous wing, trapped outside the hard-shell, caught light from the window and glowed with the iridescence of fairy wings. Her morning sickness—which was really more of a morning, afternoon, and night sickness—

brought a sour taste to her mouth. Not everyone got as sick, the doctor had said. ("Of course, not everyone's got what you've got growing inside.")

She glanced over her shoulder, through a coved archway that led to her bedroom and the tiny bathroom where Marc finished up his shower. He wanted her to call the bugman to come spray, but this time, no matter what Marc said, she would refuse.

Another cockroach, this one about as big as a pecan, crawled across the counter. Amazing beings, such cunning and timeless creatures of the dark. She had read somewhere that the cockroach was one of the few creatures to survive the Ice Age.

There were no clean bowls left in the cupboard and she pressed her belly against the counter, wishing that her arms were longer, or better yet, that Marc would offer to wash dishes. The sink was half full of water and soapsuds that had dissolved overnight, depositing a layer of scum like a temporary skin. Nose wrinkled, she forced herself to stick a hand into the water and pull up the stopper. A shiny film clung to her hand until she rinsed it clean.

After washing one porcelain bowl yellowed to the color of old bone, she started to prepare a fruit basket for Marc's breakfast. First, she rubbed a pink grapefruit clean with a paper towel, then opened the drawer and chose a small serrated knife with a handle made from polished wood. Something dark passed across the blade: the shadowy figure of a cockroach. It fell to the floor when she jerked her hand, but lay still, either stunned or trying to trick her into thinking it was dead.

From the bedroom she heard the sounds of Marc dressing: the closet door squeaking open, then slamming shut; footsteps crossing the wooden floor; a dresser drawer being scraped across its uneven tracks. The cockroach meanwhile righted itself and managed to disappear beneath the cabinets.

"Don't I have any clean socks?" Marc called.

"In the drawer," she answered and he said, "Oh."

To form the basket she cut two half circles into the top of the grapefruit rind, leaving a half-inch strip for a handle. She peeled away the bits of rind. Her eyes watered from the spray of citrus juice, yet the smell was so sweet, she thought she might have cried anyway. She scooped out the grapefruit pulp, then the white membrane, then the core, and scalloped the edge of the rind with her knife. Into the grapefruit basket she spooned a bit of grapefruit, along with leftover canned fruit cocktail, her dinner from the night before. She wiped down the blade and stowed the knife away in the drawer.

She and Marc lived in the smaller half of the shotgun double. On the other side of the kitchen wall was the landlord's bigger kitchen. The landlord had brought the bugman out to spray the roaches on his side, so for the next couple of weeks, the roaches would hide from the poison in the walls or in her cupboards. They would eat her food until the poison lost its effectiveness. Then they would flee back to the landlord's side and the cat dish that was nearly always full. The roaches usually weren't bad on her side, except for when the landlord sprayed. Roni Sue kept all the food put away and made sure the dirty dishes were always covered by water.

Live and let live, she thought. They were only bugs, and for the most part, kept out of her way. She didn't know why they bothered him so.

Marc stepped up from behind to kiss her neck. He was still a little wet from the shower and the water on his mustache tickled, cool, refreshing, unlike the warm sweat that glued her tricot slip to her skin. He moved to the side to finish buttoning his shirt and tuck the ends into the waistband of his pants.

Pointing to the grapefruit Mark said, "This for me?" He reached for it when she nodded. He asked with a weary expression, "Gonna go see the babies again, today?"

"Yes," she said, though Marc didn't know the half of it. He assumed that she was going to the postpartum ward at the hospital; it was easier letting him think this than trying to explain her fascination with the baby exhibit at the medical school. She visited the babies every day before lunch. The building was air conditioned, that was one reason, but mostly she liked to look at them, and then to think about the babies she carried, and how it would be to donate them to science. She felt them now, swimming inside her, tiny limbs folded up like frogs' legs.

Marc pulled away to grab the still-folded *Picayune* from the table. He swatted a cockroach that scurried across the counter, managing to stun it. Roni Sue watched its legs twitch; clever creature—the roach was only biding its time before turning over and scuttling away.

"Call the bugman," said Marc, his voice tight. "He hasn't come in nearly two months. Can't stand these things anymore. They're disgusting," he said, glaring at her belly. "It's gross how you can see them move," he said.

She caught the look he gave her. Why couldn't she be beautiful the way pregnant women were supposed to be? A slow breath, measured and deep—the kind of breath she hoped she could remember to use when she was in labor—helped to calm her. "Hurry," she said, "or you'll miss the trolley." She rubbed her belly. These babies had no choice but to feed on her until they were born.

Marc was still angry they were having babies they couldn't afford in the first place. Her pastor had called to talk on the phone just the other day, and when Roni Sue had carried on about Marc, her pastor had said how some men were selfish in that way. They got used to things being a certain way, they didn't want those things to change.

"Marc will learn to love his offspring once they're born," her pastor swore. "They're a part of him and he won't be able to help himself."

Roni Sue wanted to believe that. She glanced at the clock over the stove and said, "Better get a move on, if you gonna be at work on time."

Marc stomped his foot. "Yesterday, the landlord called me at work to complain about how we ain't been spraying. He told me we better take care of things if we want to renew the lease. One bedroom, Roni Sue. Place isn't gonna be big enough for all of us once those babies come, but we can't afford anything bigger on just my salary."

"Doctor says I can't work right now," she answered, wishing he would stop blaming her for everything that went wrong.

"I don't understand you, Roni Sue. What's gotten into you? Landlord pays for the bugman, so what do you care about the roaches, anyhow? Think about me for a change. Call him," Marc said, then sat down to drink chicory coffee and read the paper.

"Sure," said Roni Sue. "I'll call."

"Your babies," he had said. Not *our* babies or *my* babies. Fine. They were hers, then.

The bugman's last visit was right after they moved into the shotgun double, just before she learned that she was pregnant. He walked with a limp and carried a metal can on his back filled with poison. The can's aluminum hose attached to a black rubber nozzle that he held in his hand like a gun. The bugman was only about five-foot four, but so bent he seemed shorter.

She remembered how he squeezed the trigger to spray bitter-smelling liquid inside the drawers and under the cabinets and over the pots and pans and on the silverware and on the floors and everywhere where roaches could live, which was everywhere. For days the house smelled like it had been washed with ripe bananas mixed with grapefruit rinds, dirt and gasoline, and sweat.

"Safe as can be," he had said when she had asked about the spray. They both knew he was lying, but Roni Sue, sick with nausea, hadn't felt up to washing all the dishes after.

Three months later and her blood pressure got high enough the doctor made her quit her job. Marc said she was just being "weak," but she blamed the bugman. She had never told Marc about the ultrasound and the six fernlike babies. He thought she was carrying twins.

"Another benzene spill in the Mississippi," said Marc now, reading from the back page. "Good thing we get bottled water."

A one-inch cockroach crawled toward the crevice in the grout and Roni Sue saw it lay a turd the size of a black bean on the counter. When she looked closer she realized that it was not a turd at all, but an egg case. The coating was shiny black, round on one side with a serrated edge on the other. It was horrible, alien. She worked up the nerve to touch it.

A shiver coursed through her; she squinted, trying to see if anything moved inside. She reached up into the cupboard for an empty jar to cover the egg case, and laughed -- for all practical purposes she had made an incubator.

Marc was too preoccupied with his reading to notice, though if he had seen, he would have squashed the egg. He wasn't at all curious about babies the way she was.

She turned on the faucet, unable to remember if the water was always this gray, or if the color was darker than usual, maybe related to the spill. By the time she finished washing up, Marc was ready, at last, to go to work.

"Bye now," he said. "Remember to call the bugman. Today, and I mean it! Things don't happen unless you make them."

"Sure," she answered.

She watched him walk away. He paused outside the door and peered through the sheers covering the front window. The layers of glass and fabric distorted his face and for a moment, she imagined he was smiling. She waved and he turned away and walked across the stoop and down the stairs. This time, he kept going.

Roni Sue opened the drawer where she kept the company cards the bugman had sent out every two or three weeks to remind her that her house was overdue for a service. The cards were manila brown, with ink smeared across the bottom so she couldn't read his name. She threw them into the garbage, then walked into her bedroom.

She opened the closet and chose a dress. The dress had a ruffle at the neck and along the bottom of the sleeves and at the bodice. The ruffles were humiliating decorations, but it took too much money to buy stylish maternity clothes. It seemed bad enough that she was fat as an elephant—in this dress she looked ridiculous, a ruffled blimp.

She slid her purse strap over her shoulder and walked out to the stoop. Just about the only way to get on her shoes anymore was to sit on the glider and swing her legs up, one at a time. She had to rest for a few seconds after that, and took her time walking up General Pershing Street, and across St. Charles to the Neutral Zone, where the streetcar stopped on its way downtown.

On the ground, a crumpled *Picayune,* with a briny smell that hadn't yet warmed enough to turn rotten. Tucked inside were broken crawfish shells, discarded by someone too lazy to walk an extra yard to the garbage can.

She shuddered. How Marc loved crawfish, loved sucking out the sweet fatty flesh from their shells. The thought of it all made her sick and she found herself sweating so hard her hair clung to her head like a lead cap.

A small boy stared at her belly and tugged on his mother's shirtsleeve. "What's she got in her?" he asked, and the mother scowled.

She picked her boy up and said, "Shush, now. Don you axt about such tings."

Then the streetcar came and the driver didn't even wait for her to sit on the wood bench before he clanged his bell and started off. A drunkard stumbled in beside her and pressed one thick thigh up against hers. He looked at her belly and moved to the other side of the streetcar. The windows were open, but the air was too thick for any exchange to take place, so it was almost worse than it was outside, where at least she could have moved.

She rode, each bump sending her compressed bladder into spasm. Her uterus pushed on her bladder; the doctor had said it might stay this way until she delivered. These were parts of her body that she had never thought about before now. She was all connected, just like her house without its hallways.

It took about twenty minutes to get downtown. At last the streetcar stopped on Canal Street and Roni Sue hurried past the shoppers and cut through an alley that ended across the street from the entrance to the Tulane Medical School. She strolled in, trying to look as if she belonged there. "I have an appointment with the Dean," she would say, if anyone asked why she was there, though so far, no one ever had.

The air conditioning sandwiched her in front and in back and because she was dripping with sweat, for the first time all day, she felt chilled. Her skin tingled as if she had been splashed with an astringent. Her face flushed hot and she took the elevator up to the third floor to see the babies. The third floor held the medical education offices, but by now, everyone there had gone out for lunch; in the empty hallway, her steps echoed off the shiny linoleum. She turned the corner and stood before the display case along the wall.

A pathologist who once lectured at the medical school had set up the baby exhibit. The bugman first told her about the collection, said one of his children was there, but didn't say which one it was.

Now, every day, she went to stare through the glass windows at shelves filled with glass jars filled to the brim with formaldehyde-soaked fetuses. She couldn't really tell, could only imagine what they must smell like. There were over twenty specimens; she could never figure out which one belonged to the bugman. Sometimes she wondered if she should try harder to shake her fascination with nature's mistakes.

So many things could go wrong. Intuitively, she had known it all along. She looked at the first jar, an anencephalic monster, whose skin was luminous and gray, with loose folds bunched up around the back and neck. There were indentations for the eyes, but no forehead and no back of the head, just a concave skull like an empty bowl to showcase smooth gray brains. It reminded her of the grapefruit basket she had fixed for Marc, or maybe it was the other way around, maybe she had fixed the grapefruit basket to remind herself of the fetus.

Then there were the Siamese Twins and on the next shelf, the triplet specimens, still connected by macerated umbilical cords. It made her want to cry to think of how their fates were intertwined. She felt something crawl inside her belly and without meaning to, reached forward to place her hand against the window.

"Poor babies," she said, ready to cry. "I would never ever do this to you, never put you on display." As if to answer, the glass vibrated beneath her touch and she heard the echo of uneven steps and liquid sloshing against metal and the ripe banana and citrus smell. She stopped breathing, wondering if it was the bugman, there to visit his baby. She watched a shadow turn the corner, but before he could see her, she ran to the end of the hall and ducked behind a door leading to the stairwell.

Was the bugman trying to be a good daddy?

She listened to his voice, scratchy and off-key, as he stood before the glass case, singing a lullaby. "You'll have company soon, my boy," he said, then chuckled. "Yessiree, we'll get you some new friends to play with. Twins, I think, from the look of things."

Her stomach bolted and she turned and rushed for the exit and opened the door to the stairwell.

"He's the monster," she said, not quite to herself, maybe to her babies. She made her way down the steps, unable to run because you couldn't run with a belly that big and your feet hidden from view. She pushed open the fire door and left the building. The whooshing of her pulse in her ears sounded like the bugman's footsteps. Then again, it was hot enough to hallucinate, to misinterpret whispers for threats. She started to laugh. Well it was normal, wasn't it, for a pregnant lady to feel a little spooked now and then?

Outside, the heat seemed to swarm around her like a zillion tiny flies. The day was far enough along that her ankles swelled and her bladder hurt and it seemed to take forever to get to the streetcar. There, it was so crowded she had to stand most of the way home. Finally she reached her stop. She hurried back to her place, where she fumbled with the keys. Her bladder sent a sharp pain through her abdomen and she didn't care when the door didn't latch, she was in such a hurry. She passed through the living room and into the kitchen and into the bedroom and the bathroom.

When she went back into the kitchen, she looked at her mason jar and noticed that the egg case had hatched. There were thirty or more little babies, tiny dark things with hair-thin legs and see-though baby wings. She watched them climb up the jar, looking for a way out. In an hour or so, a couple of the smaller babies began to eat the egg case, while some of the bigger ones began to eat each other.

So that's how it was—just like she had always heard it—only the strong survived.

She put her hand on her belly, but couldn't tell if the babies were kicking or if it was just her high blood pressure pushing fluid around inside. She pictured the jar babies at the medical center and remembered how the bugman swore his spray didn't do anything to harm her baby. "Had six kids myself," he had said, "and only one of them died. Good thing for that," he said, "Cause we couldn't afford no more hungry little mouths, anyway."

She would never forget the look on her doctor's face when the tech had called him in to view the ultrasound. "My God," he had said, looking away, though Roni Sue had not been able to take her eyes off of her babies.

"They're beautiful," she had answered in amazement. "The way they move like ferns, like there's a wind blowing them from behind. So delicate. Why look at them, they're dancing."

The doctor tried to get her to have an abortion, just like Marc had done the second he learned about the pregnancy, but she had said no.

Now it was too late, much too late. She was having these babies no matter what anyone said, no matter how many times the doctor talked to her of "understanding through research." She had stopped going to the doctor. When the babies came, she would have them at home, where they'd be safe, where she could protect them.

The telephone rang—Marc. "Just called the bugman," he said. "He's on his way. I'm warning you, Roni Sue. I can't stand the way things are starting to look around home. You best be listening if you know what's good for us." She heard him slam down the phone.

So many things could go wrong, she thought, and most of them were things you could do nothing to prevent. Things like finally getting pregnant after so many years of trying, things like having your blood pressure boil and benzene spills in the drinking water. Things like getting fat and having your husband grow out of love.

She thought about the baby with the grapefruit head and prayed to God her babies wouldn't ever end up in someone else's collection. So many things could go wrong, but at least, because of the baby exhibit, Roni Sue knew what to expect.

The doorbell chimed and even before she stepped through into the living room, she smelled him—the bugman—his metal can filled with poison. She stood frozen, staring at him through the sheers. He waved and pushed open the unlocked door. He peeked around inside. The bugman nodded and tipped his cap. "Afternoon," he said. "You didn't return my calls. That don't matter because your husband called instead." He smiled at her with tobacco-stained teeth.

As he scurried past her the liquid in the can gurgled. He looked around with a frown on his face and squashed a fat roach sunbathing in the middle of the kitchen floor. He dragged his foot away, leaving a brown streak across the linoleum. He pressed the trigger to spray the roach he had already killed.

"Pretty lady," he said. "You shouldn't have let things go on so long." He shook his head and that was when she noticed the tremor that rocked the top half of his body. "It's hard to control them when they've had this long to breed." He licked his lips, then aimed the nozzle to spray beside the refrigerator.

"Stop," she said, "no more," but he didn't listen.

"Your husband's the one who called," he said. "Your husband, he's my boss now, not you."

Roni Sue watched the bugman spray the utensils in the dish strainer. He sprayed the glassware; opened drawers and sprayed; lifted up the paper lining in the cabinets and sprayed; sprayed the sink and around the drain, where the poison would be washed into the sewers and eventually end up in the Mississippi. It was all connected, she thought, just like their shotgun double.

"What's this?" he asked, noticing the jar, which now housed only the few baby roaches that had survived eating the others. He gave her a puzzled look like he was humoring her. He licked his lips, then sprayed a circle around the jar. "Nowhere to run," said the bugman with a laugh. He wiped his nose, then wiped his hands on his pants. He looked at her feet, and she worried he would spray a circle around her.

His wide grin made his lips all but disappear. "Guess I better come back every few weeks till we get things under control. If that's not enough, you just be sure to call and I'll be right over," he said.

She held her breath as she waited for him to leave. When he had gone, she opened all the windows. A fat roach lay on the counter on its back, its legs bent in spasm. She picked it up and threw it out the window, hopeful it could still recover. She thought of how the cockroaches always came to her side whenever the bugman sprayed the landlord's kitchen. Even now, she heard them crawling in the walls, just waiting until it was safe to come out again. Maybe that's what I should do, she thought, hide away in a crevice, and wait for the poison to die down.

It was all so very funny when she thought about it. She stood rocking herself, arms folded gently across her belly. A laugh bubbled up and in a moment she was laughing uncontrollably, tears of joy trickling over her eyelids and down cheeks. She grabbed hold of the counter, trying to calm herself enough to catch her breath.

Something sharp poked her from inside, an elbow, or a knee. Her lips were numb and one eyelid pulled up in a tic and all at once Roni Sue no longer felt like laughing. The poison couldn't hurt her babies any longer; what was done was done.

From habit, she opened the drawer and looked at the cutlery as she thought about what to make for dinner. Her hand closed in around the smooth handle of the serrated knife and she lifted the knife to search for the reflection of her face in the blade.

Tiny veins had broken beneath her pale skin, the blood fanning out like sunburst. Marc was all wrong. She looked beautiful, radiant, just as the ladies at church had always said.

She turned on the water to rinse the poison from the knife. When something tickled from inside she put down the knife to rub her belly. My, but those critters were active today. The feeling of love she felt for her babies overwhelmed her.

"Now, now," she said to her babies. "Don't you worry. Everything is going to be all right, you'll see."

Even with the windows open, the air in the kitchen was stifling. The bitter smell of pesticide made her stomach queasy. She poured herself a tall glass of weak ice tea to take out to the stoop.

Careful not to spill, she eased into the cushions. The glider cushions smelled sour, but the odor was so familiar it didn't bother her. Roni Sue fluffed up a pillow, kicked off her shoes, and sat back. The glider moved with only the slightest of effort, and the constant rocking, rocking, rocking threatened to put her to sleep.

Then a mosquito whined from somewhere behind her, and she turned, trying to spot it. With all that humidity—and the air as thick as a damp wool coat—she should have seen the ripple of the mosquito flapping its wings. But nothing moved, at least nothing she could see, and before she knew it, she had dozed off.

A fat moth woke her up with its knocking against the window; she opened her eyes to the dark. Inside, her house glowed from the yellow light of the kitchen. Marc must have been working late again. Fine by her. At dusk the world was not quite black and not quite white—like looking at an old TV.

She kept the glider moving, thinking she would stay on the porch for as long as it took for Marc to come home so she could tell him about her day. She wanted to tell Marc all about the babies and the bugman and the trolley. She wanted to tell him, though she knew Marc could have cared less. Marc thought her weak, but once she had the babies, Roni Sue would prove how the strong sometimes survived just by waiting.

One more month to go. After those babies were born, she would love them no matter how they turned out. More important than that, her babies would love her. Marc might not feel that way any longer, but soon that wouldn't matter.

There would be lots of *them* soon enough, and only one of Marc. She patted her belly and smiled. The waiting wasn't so bad when you had something wonderful to look forward to.

THE COST OF DOING BUSINESS

First Appeared in *Amazing Stories*, copyright 1999,
reprinted in *Nebula Awards 2000*, edited by Robert Silverberg

The big man sits across from Zita, brow furrowed, black eyes fixed upon the desk. He strokes the mahogany finish while he's talking, touching it rather absently, as if trying to smooth things out. Every now and again he glances up to make certain Zita is still paying attention to his story. There are two thugs outside, waiting for him in the parking lot. Can he hire her to take his place, deal with the thugs, so he won't have to? There isn't much time to decide, and certainly, from his view, no choice.

Zita scribbles a few notes. She is grateful he doesn't stare at her like a lot of customers, who give her an I-can't-believe-I'm-really-here look and expect her to find their naiveté charming. When customers stare at her long legs or dress cut low to expose skin smooth as a white chocolate shell, it isn't really Zita they are seeing. Her perfection is only skin-deep, skin-deep being all anyone can afford, even the big man.

She notices his gold Rolex and his suit sewn from fine wool. Like her, the big man wears his riches on the outside.

"This is the worst thing that's ever happened to me," the big man blathers. "At first I didn't know what to do, but then I looked up, saw your billboard. That's why I'm here."

Driving to work this morning he was carjacked. "I'm a lucky man," he says, really lucky. The thugs were curious types;

they agreed to let him hire a surrogate victim in exchange for an extra couple of bills and a contract promising immunity. That's the way things are done these days, when people act reasonably. Fortunately for the big man, the thugs are reasonable men.

Zita listens as he prattles off twenty reasons why he needs to hire her instead of facing things on his own. She's tempted to correct him, but doesn't. The excuses are all part of the game. She knows why he wants to hire her, has known from the moment he walked into her office. It has nothing to do with his suspicious wife, or a job he can't afford to take time off from, or even his heart condition. Sure, the big man is afraid of pain—who isn't? —but there's more to it than that. The big man has sought Zita's services for the same reason as everyone who hires a surrogate victim. He'd rather see someone else suffer.

Something terrible has happened to him; he can't turn back the clock, so he might as well make the best of it. He won't admit that there's a reason he'll pay a premium to hire her instead of that balding Mr. Tompkins on the second floor: hiring a young woman instead of a middle-aged man makes the deal a little sweeter.

The transaction is completely legal, but the big man feels enough shame about his cowardice that he works himself into a sweat; he pauses to dab his forehead with a handkerchief. When he brings it away, his brow is still furrowed. The wrinkles on his face are set, like a shirt doomed for the rag bin. He looks around the room, paying attention to his surroundings for the first time.

She's decorated well out front. Out here, where she shows her public face it's perfect. The walls are painted a fleshy tone called "Peach Fizz." Her costumes are one-of-a-kind and are displayed in a glass case. The overstuffed chairs are from Ethan Allen, with top-of-the-line fabrics that the sales associate promised could take a lot of abuse. Her desk is an eighteenth-century French copy, and there are several abstract oils she bought at an uptown gallery, all by the same artist, someone kind of famous, (though not so much as to be overpriced) whose name she can't ever remember. She doesn't understand abstract painting; it's just that realism bothers her.

Her office is nothing like the back room where she lives. There, the floors are scratched and bare, save for the ripped mattress where she sleeps. Paint peels from the walls like skin from an old sunburn. On the small table where she takes her meals sits a memorial shrine dedicated to her daughter. There's a gold-rimmed snapshot, surrounded by dried wreaths and flowers, plastic beads, a favorite book. A shower takes up a quarter of the room; a small refrigerator covers what would otherwise be the counter space and that's okay. She doesn't need much room and she doesn't want much counter space. Anything that can't be eaten cold right out of the container isn't worth eating.

Just then the telephone rings, and the big man says, "Aren't you going to get that?"

It's probably some idiot calling to ask if she'll have her pants pulled down in front of a minister, or if she'll let some guy's boss chew her out in front of all his coworkers. "Popcorn" is what surrogates call the little jobs. Things that fill up space without having much substance. She takes on popcorn occasionally, when she's in the right mood, but usually refers little jobs to a girl she met one time when she was in the hospital. That girl is in a bad way and needs all the help she can get. Besides, Zita finds the big jobs much more satisfying.

"Well," the big man prompts. The phone annoys him; he's the type who would be annoyed by interruptions.

Eventually, the machine picks up, just as she knew it would. "A true emergency would walk right in without making an appointment. The way you did," she explains.

He nods and she can tell he likes being thought of as a true emergency.

"Anything else you want to tell me?" she says.

"Yeah. These guys are armed. One has a metal pipe and a gun, the other a long knife."

"Sounds doable."

"So, how much do you charge?" he asks, somewhat timidly.

She expects him to say, "I've never done this before." They often say that, even when she knows it isn't true.

The big man doesn't say it, but she knows that's what he's thinking. She takes her time before quoting a price. The only reason to ask for more than she needs is to impress upon customers the value of her service. She doesn't really care about the money; she's not in business for that. There are a hundred Licensed Surrogates in her state. She doubts if one of them cares about money. No amount could make up for what she goes through every day, what they all go through. She states her fee. "My standard rate," she says. "Plus expenses."

"You'll take it all? Everything they dish out?" he asks.

She nods. That's what she does. She takes it all, every bit of it, so that important people like the big man can avoid suffering.

He reaches into his coat pocket for his wallet and his credit card. "Those guys looked pretty mean. There might be scarring."

"Those are the expenses."

They both laugh, but his is more like a grunt. The whole experience must be quite a strain on his heart: his breathing quickens, his lips fade to a powdery blue. When the card changes hands his fingers leave a cold residue that makes her want more than anything to duck into the back room for a shower. Stop it, she tells herself. Disgust is not professional.

"What would you like me to wear?" she asks.

He stands and faces the glass case. Her sequined gown has a rip and is being repaired, but otherwise, everything is there.

"The white leather coveralls," he says after a while.

"Nothing underneath. And don't zip it up all the way. Leave a little cleavage. Not too much, just a shadow. Ladylike, not slutty."

His face turns ruddy and she knows he would like her to disrobe in front of him. Not my job, she thinks. Not my job.

"If you'll excuse me." She opens the display case and holds the coveralls against her, giving him a moment to reconsider his choice.

"That will be fine," he says.

Zita smiles a professional smile, then steps into the backroom to change.

She takes the big man's arm and leads him through the hallway to the rear staircase. They walk down to the first floor. "Were there protestors out today?" she asks, gesturing over her shoulder toward the front.

"I didn't see any when I pulled into the lot," he says. "I hope there isn't trouble. I don't want trouble. Or publicity."

"Listen," she says, "if they weren't out front they certainly won't be out back. There's no point in protesting unless someone sees you. These guys don't care about morality— they only want it to look like they do."

"Okay," he says, not sounding convinced.

They open the fire door and step onto the parking lot.

The sun hides behind thin clouds, yet the day is muggy and bright. If the sun were out it would be blinding, one of those days when you can't even look at the ground without squinting. Zita sees the perps inside what she guesses must be his car. Black Beamer—sunroof—leather interior. They walk closer.

The big man realizes that the seats have been slashed. He groans.

"They can be replaced," she says.

He answers, "Yeah, but still."

"Forget it," she says. "Just think of it as the cost of doing business."

"Easy for you to say," says the big man.

"Easy?" she says, and stops walking. "Easy?" Just what does he think this is? He's even more of a jerk than she imagined.

He must realize his faux pas for he looks at his feet and says, "Sorry. Come on. Let's get this over with. The big man calls out to the perps in the car, "Here she is." He speaks quickly; he is very anxious to put this all behind him. "You boys remember our deal, now."

The one who must be the leader opens the front door and steps out. He holds a pistol, aims it toward Zita.

He's short and his hair is black and nicely cut. He reminds her of a philosophy student: jeans, a plaid flannel shirt, clean shoes. His partner is skinny, with sunken eyes like a twenty-four-hour bruise. The partner is dressed more slovenly—maybe he's majoring in political science—in a dirty tee shirt and torn pants.

She notices that the big man has silently dropped back behind her. Good, she thinks. Better he stay out of her way.

"Give him his stuff," she tells the thugs. "You can have the money and you can have me. He just wants what belongs to him."

A parking lot attendant, wearing earphones, approaches.

Because she doesn't recognize him she guesses that he's new here. Zita reaches into her pocket to flash her license.

He stops, rubs his neck as if trying to remember what he has been told about such things at the orientation. At last it hits him: she's a surrogate, just doing her job. The attendant salutes. "Sorry to intrude," he says, and walks back to his booth.

She replaces her license, tucks it between the few bills she carries for show.

"Shit!" says the skinny partner, looking about. He's nervous.

It's nice to know, she thinks, that you can be a total jerk as long as you still feel nervous.

"I don't know if I like this," he says. "Maybe we shouldn't have let him talk us into this."

For a second the leader looks like he might agree with his sidekick, but when the big man says, "Don't forget you signed a contract. I'll press charges if you don't hold up your end of the deal," bravado washes over him; he swaggers away from the car like the bad guy in a western.

The big man pushes Zita forward. "The briefcase," he

whispers. "Tell them not to scuff it."

"What makes you think I won't kill you both?" asks the leader. He waves his gun in an arc.

The big man gasps, and Zita turns to glare at him, warning him to stay calm. She's the one they want to see acting scared, not him. It's her job now. She knows from experience that if the big man screams or acts stupid he'll just mess things up. "Relax," she barks. They have a contract. Life is not the free-for-all some people assume it is. The majority abides by the rules. After all, what would become of society if everyone changed things willy-nilly?

"Don't forget your agreement," she says. "He doesn't want any trouble."

"Maybe I want trouble," says the leader.

"That's why I'm here," Zita says. "Go ahead, scumbag, take it out on me. Think of all the bitches you've known who have led you on, but in the end decided they were too good for you. Bitches who made you beg for affection, then denied you what you deserved, what you needed. Think of what you would have done to them if they hadn't managed to get away." She takes a step closer. "Give him his stuff. Take it out on me," she says again.

Her statement has the impact she is aiming for. He grimaces and a tic starts near his upper lip. "Stay there!" he says to his partner. "Me first." He tosses the car keys to the pavement. The big man stoops to grab them, scurries out of the way. The leader stands before her. His breath is sweet, like he's just sucked on a peppermint. She doesn't know why, but this strikes her as funny. Before she can stop herself she is giggling.

"Bitch!" he says. "What are you laughing at?" He slaps her face and slaps it again and again until she cries out. The one time she couldn't change places and ease someone else's suffering was when her daughter died.

Now, he is grinding his prick against her belly and squeezing her tit hard enough to sting.

She feels the big man watching her.

"No!" she cries out. There was nothing she could have done, only there was, and she knows it.

He takes the pistol and brings it down hard on her head.

It wasn't safe to let the girl outside unsupervised, but he said, "Forget about the kid," and she said, "Okay," and now her baby was dead and no amount of grief could bring her back.

The pistol strikes again.

She feels terror this man might hurt her more than they usually do. There's a gleam in his eye, like he doesn't care whether she's dead or alive when it comes time to rape her. "Please," she says. They always like it when she begs, but that's not why she asks for mercy. The pain has become unbearable. She can no longer tell the ground from the sky. She stumbles and falls. With her ear pressed against the asphalt she thinks she hears the big man's heavy breath.

The leader kicks her in the small of her back, says, "Get up."

She screams as the heel of his boot knocks into her face. Her daughter, drowned, and her inside, making it with a guy who still denies he was the father.

Oh God, it should have been me, she thinks. Oh God, it should have been me.

When Zita comes to she's in her usual suite at the hospital.

A nurse says dryly, "Good. You're back from the dead," as she injects some white fluid from a vial into the IV. The nurse writes something on a chart before offering Zita a brown plastic cup filled with water.

Zita tries to say thanks, but her throat feels like there are a dozen razor blades propping it open. She's thirsty, but too afraid to drink, so shakes her head no. The movement brings on a pounding pain and makes everything blurry.

Next, the doctor struts into the room and reads the notes on the chart before acknowledging her. "You again," he says. He yawns. "You're sending both my kids to college. Private. Out of state. You know that, don't you?" He winks at the nurse, then they both laugh. He sidles up near Zita's face to shine a penlight in her eyes. He presses his fingers against her neck. "We almost lost you this time. Did it hurt?" he asks.

"Not enough," she answers.

He takes a mirror from the bedside stand to let her see his handiwork.

The face staring back in the mirror looks vaguely familiar, like someone she's only seen from far away.

"Looking good," the doctor says, "better than new. Give it a week for the swelling to go down. Oh, and I had to replace a hip, so go easy on jogging."

A sharp pain shoots from her jaw up through her cheek. She groans. "Doctor, can you please give me an injection?"

"I thought you liked the pain," says the doctor.

"Think what you like," Zita says. Even the hospital staff wants to see her suffer, wants to see her beg. Ironic that she must pay them for the privilege. "Give me a shot."

"Well, I suppose she can have some morphine," says the doctor. "Five milligrams IV now. Every four hours PRN, until tomorrow. After that, she can take codeine. Wouldn't want her to get too dependent," he says.

An orderly walks in, bearing an obscenely big flower arrangement. It's too large to go on the bedside stand and the orderly sets it on the floor beside the wall. He reads her the card without asking if she cares who sent the flowers.

They're from the big man. Pale yellow roses with sprigs of freesia the color of bruises. How sweet.

In a couple of days they send her out to finish her recovery at home. The bed is there for someone who really needs it, not for someone who simply wants it.

"Always a pleasure," says the doctor with a wave. "See you in a couple of months."

She ignores him and asks the nurse to call her a cab.

The nurse makes Zita sit in a green vinyl wheelchair, despite her assertion that she is well enough to walk. "You want to walk out of here like a normal human being you gotta walk in like one, too," says the nurse.

Zita shrugs, and lowers herself into the chair. She has no change of clothes and must wear her coveralls, now caked with blood that's gone black. The nurse sets the heavy flower arrangement in Zita's lap, and wheels her down the hallway to the exit.

Once outside an angry woman in a tailored black pants suit accosts them, who waves a placard in front of her face that says, "OUTLAW SURROGATE VICTIMS NOW!"

There's a camera crew, who rushes in to catch the shot.

"How can you do this?" the woman screams at Zita.

"How can you let these perverts abuse you so? It has to end! What you're doing is against God! This madness has got to stop!"

The woman keeps screaming as she follows Zita to the taxi. "You're nothing but an overpriced whore!" she says. "Whore!"

The cabby takes the flowers and opens her door so Zita can get in. He sets the flowers on the seat beside her. He shoos away the protester with a practiced wave, elbows the cameraman in the ribs. He hurries to get behind the wheel. "Time is money," says the cabby, revving up the engine. "Where to, Miss Whore?" Without waiting for her to answer he pulls away from the lot.

"Very funny," she says. She tells him the address of her office. It hurts a bit to talk, but otherwise she feels pretty good. It's amazing, she thinks, how quickly the body heals.

"So, uh, you're one of them surrogate victims, huh? Not sure how I feel about those. More I think about it, more I tend to agree with that lady back there. Maybe the whole business ought to be illegal. Maybe we shouldn't let people like you do what you are doing."

"It would be like it was during Prohibition," Zita says. "A wasted effort. Couldn't stop it then. Can't stop it now."

"I get your point all right, but that's no reason to give up," says the cabby. "Just because you can't get rid of all evil doesn't mean you can't get rid of some of it. You gotta start somewhere, don't you think? Gotta try. Otherwise, where would we be? You know, society. Culture."

"I never thought of it like that," she says. There's no point in arguing with the cabby. She could make him feel bad by telling him that she makes a hundred times what he does, maybe then he would understand, or at least think he did.

They drive on, painfully silent like they are in a room where someone is expected to die. The cabby lets her out in the alley and stays seated behind the wheel. She braces the flowers, between her good hip and the car door, gives the cabby a big enough tip to make him blush.

"Been nice talking to you," she says, then opens the door and steps out.

"Likewise," answers the cabby. Unlike her, he probably means it. He pulls away without waiting to see if she can walk to her building.

Zita leaves the flower arrangement on the stoop for the homeless lady who lives by the trash bin. She tucks the last of her money inside the card. She manages to climb up the steps to her place, where she plans to sleep until her prescription for pain runs dry. She hangs the closed sign on the door. She's exhausted. Maybe by next week she'll be ready to listen to her messages, choose her next job. Something easy, mindless. A prank or some simple humiliation. Popcorn.

It feels good to be home. In her "kitchen" she pours a cheap bourbon into a chipped coffee cup that says World's Greatest Mom. She doesn't much like the stuff because it burns, but she can't see paying extra just to get something that goes down smooth. With the door that leads to her office closed she can hardly hear the phone ring. When it keeps on ringing she figures out that the answering machine is full. They've got a lot of nerve calling the minute she gets out of the hospital. Let them wait.

Zita pours herself another shot. It's like drinking lukewarm fire and doesn't quite do the trick. She has another drink, but the phone is still ringing and the only way to make it stop is to pull out the plug.

Even if no one else can understand the why of it, Zita knows with all her heart that being a professional victim is the right thing to do.

So the protestors think she should stop. She has no use for the rhetoric of do-gooders. What do they know? She is a professional victim. No matter what she does she's going to suffer for the rest of her life in ways no one can even imagine. Her baby is dead; she has no choice but to suffer.

Assholes like the doctor and the nurse and the cabby and the zealot with her sign—they just want her to give it away for free.

FRANKENFETISH

The three of us sat at the table pretending everything was normal. I poured water into a jam jar for Daddy and milk into plastic mugs for Wendell and me. Daddy asked God to bless both children before dishing out scoops of macaroni and cheese, the third night in a row. It was Wendell's week to make dinner. When I'd made macaroni and cheese on Friday, I'd also prepared a red cabbage salad, but Wendell was afraid to dig around in the refrigerator drawers and find a side dish, so this was a one-dish meal. Wendell's hair was orangier than our dinner. Some girl called him a carrot top, but that didn't make any sense, not that I'd seen any carrots lately, but weren't their tops green? My plate had a black hairline fracture running through the center of porcelain the color of a lightly scrambled egg. I was tired of eating things made from noodles. I was too hungry not to eat.

"How was school?" Daddy asked.

I said fine, even though it wasn't.

Wendell got started about his foursquare game and how there were fleas living in his best friend Joey Bickell's socks.

"Do we have to hear this at dinner?" I asked. I was wearing the purple sundress that used to be Mama's. It almost fit—except around the shoulders and waist. I had hemmed the skirt just above the knees because I knew how to do hems. My hair was pulled up into a bun that the school bus driver said made me look sophisticated.

Daddy held up his hand like a crossing guard. "It's okay, Lola," he said. "Let him talk."

Since I was the mature child, I did. I wanted to please Daddy even though I could hardly wait to get into the laboratory and see if Mama's tumor had grown since last night. It wasn't the whole tumor, just a clump of cells he had rescued from the hospital. We kept her in a Petri dish in the laboratory. It wasn't really a laboratory. It was the wet bar in the corner of our family room. But anyone who saw it would say that it looked official, like something from a Frankenstein movie. Glass cabinets were bracketed to the walls and stacked with Petri dishes full of cells. A little refrigerator with a yellow sticker in the center warned, "Not For Human Consumption." Daddy had brought home the sticker and most of our supplies from work.

"We learned at school that cows have more than one stomach," Wendell said.

"They're called ruminants," I said, prepared to explain that cows ate their own cud, but hoping no one asked me what a cud was.

"Runiments," Wendell said. He liked to pretend he understood more than he did. When he finally got done boring us with his life story, I asked, "How was work, Daddy?" and Wendell looked more disappointed than the last rat through a maze for not thinking to ask that question himself.

"Work was fine," Daddy said. He worked in Refuse Services at the hospital.

"That's nice," I said.

"Yeah, nice," said Wendell. He had pale freckles like raw sesame seeds and hair coarser than the stuff inside Daddy's nose. He was short and muscular, and looked the way you'd think a Butch ought to look instead of a Wendell. His teachers probably thought he was cute. I knew better. I knew Wendell wasn't going to be cute for very much longer and I felt really sorry for him. Because once you stopped being cute you had to be something better to get attention.

Intelligent.

Mature.

Wendell was neither.

Daddy was still wearing his faded blue coveralls—his glasses were streaked with something white. Since Mama died, Daddy had grown more and more sloppy about his appearance. Right now needed a shower. Gray bags shadowed his eyes and his chin was as dark and stubby as the teddy bear butt Wendell had shaved last week—to see if the hair would grow back.

"Find any new specimens in the incinerator?" I asked. "A few cells. They might be too contaminated to work with, but I'll do what I can," Daddy said.

"That's all you can do," I said.

Wendell nodded, as if he understood.

As if.

Daddy got a serious look on his face. "We have to deal with what we're given," he said.

"Even me?" asked Wendell.

"Even you," said Daddy.

Wendell bubbled spit into his palm, then wiped down his cowlick. Today at school, a second grader had teased him about his red hair. "Can I dye my hair?" he asked. "Black?"

"No," Daddy said.

"You should let him," I said. I figured the dye would turn his hair green. "Is everyone finished?" I asked. I stood to carry my plate to the sink. Daddy had promised I could feed the tumor after all the chores, so I was really excited. I tried not to show my feelings because excitement was so immature. Tonight was the first time Daddy was allowing me to touch one of his experiments. I was a fifth grader now, and old enough to handle the responsibility.

"Can I have seconds?" Wendell asked.

Daddy nodded and served him another scoop.

Wendell had been Mama's favorite when she was alive. That didn't help him now. Daddy was too smart to be fooled by little boy tricks. Daddy never said how Wendell's freckles were so adorable, how Wendell was good-natured—dogs are good-natured!—how comforting it was to hold little Wendell on his lap. Daddy refused to play favorites with us. I respected that.

"There are many factors required for growth," Daddy said beginning his nightly lecture. He wanted to teach us all he knew about science, which was a lot. Otherwise, he said, we were helpless to exercise control over our lives. "Nutrients. Water. Oxygen," Daddy said. "And that essence of life that I've only just recently discovered."

"Will you name your new discovery after me?" I said.

"I could call it 'Lolerium,'" Daddy said with a wink.

"No!" Wendell cried. "Wendellerium!"

"Or maybe just 'Delirium,'" I said.

Daddy looked like he was trying not to laugh. "My precocious little daughter," he said. He stood up to reach for the box of sugar cubes he kept up on the refrigerator, and added his special vitamin drops before passing them around. He hoped the drops would keep us from getting cancer. "Dessert?" he said.

I closed my mouth around my sugar cube and waited for it to soften. I made the hole grow wider, using my tongue as a poker, then sucked until the sweetness leaked out and the syrup coated my mouth like paint. The shell collapsed and all that was left were a few sandy grains. It wasn't much of a dessert, but you had to deal with what you got.

"Don't forget your promise, Daddy," I said, and Daddy answered, "I won't, Lola. Now, go on and do your chores."

Since it had been Wendell's night to cook, I got stuck doing all the dishes. The worst thing about eating macaroni and cheese was the dishes. I cleared the table while Wendell went to do his reading homework and Daddy left to take his constitutional. Wendell had scalded the milk blacker than a polished coffin and the wet cheese stuck to my sponge like snot. Scrubbing the pot clean was almost impossible. I thought about throwing it away. Except that Daddy might find out what I had done when he needed that pot, which he sometimes used to store spare parts from his experiments. Instead, I shoved the pot in the back of the cabinet by the stove, where it would be hard to find. It might take a couple of weeks before anybody even noticed. By then, I could blame it on Wendell because Daddy would never remember when we'd last used that pot, plus, Wendell wasn't nearly so good a liar as me.

I hurried out to finish my other chores.

"How are you kids coming along?" Daddy asked.

"Just fine," I said. "Just fine."

Wendell had bathroom and laundry duty, meaning it was my turn to straighten the family room. I emptied all the garbage into a black plastic bag, carried Daddy's beer cans to the porch to be recycled. When I finished I saw that Wendell was done with his homework but still hadn't started on his chores. "Hurry up!" I said.

He stuck out his tongue and walked as slow as a three-legged cat to the bathroom.

"You're so immature!" I said. The chores weren't even that bad. Daddy just wanted us to keep things cleaned up so that the odors wouldn't get out of hand. So that the neighbors wouldn't call the police. Again. I didn't want the neighbors to snoop inside our house and whisper that Daddy had a fetish about death. It wasn't true. Even if I didn't know what a fetish was, I knew it wasn't true.

The laboratory/family room was my favorite place in the house and I wanted to keep it clean. With the drapes taped shut and the lights off, the room got Movie Theater dark, the way it gets just before the show's about to start. Sometimes late at night, when everyone else was asleep, I sneaked into the family room, let my eyes adjust to the blackness, waited until I saw that it wasn't completely dark, just almost, and I could see stars on our walls. The "stars" came from Daddy's tumor collection, glowing faintly, like they had been dusted with the blue part of fire. They were all so beautiful they made me cry with joy.

The night before yesterday, I had fallen asleep on the couch with the patchwork comforter over me and a warm jar cradled in my arms. Mama's jar. When Daddy found me in the morning his eyelashes were wet, like spider webs covered with dew. He took Mama away and said, "It's better for her to be refrigerated." The jiggle of the fluid made it sound like she was singing him a song. It had been a long time since we had heard Mama sing to us. I wanted to cry.

Daddy kissed the outside of the jar before putting it away.

I didn't get into trouble and I was glad. I would have felt so alone without that little bit of Mama still living with us. We all would.

I got done sweeping the carpet, then dusted the mantel and the glass shelves, careful not to touch the Petri dish with some of Mama's gray tumor growing inside it. Taped to the wall was a hand-lettered sign Daddy had made that said, "Don't throw out the bath water with the baby."

Daddy had changed into his scientist's white coveralls and yellow rubber gloves and thick plastic goggles that made him look like a retard. I helped him roll down his sleeves. Even when he wasn't dressed for work he could have used someone sophisticated to help pick out his clothes.

From the bathroom, I heard Wendell complaining. "Yuck! It stinks worse than a refrigerator-full of dead grandmothers."

I laughed and said, "You ought to know."

That made Wendell whine even more. In a while I heard him scream, "That does it! I quit! I'm not going to stick my hand down there!" and I knew he had accidentally dropped something into the toilet, probably the sponge.

I pretended not to hear him yelling while working on a stack of magazines that needed straightening. *The Ladie's Home Journal* still got delivered to our house, not that anyone read them. I tidied those up and was searching for something else to do when I noticed Daddy watching me. His gloves were covered with clear slime; he cocked his head to look at some Petri dishes stacked on the counter-top that were awaiting insemination with the spores. He looked at me, blinked about a hundred times in a row, his "Bambi-eyes" blink that reminded me of a cartoon. He held up his glistening gloves and begged, "Lola, please!"

"I'm not finished with my chores," I said, but nobody, especially me, could resist Daddy's Bambi-eyes.

"That's okay. You can quit for now. Please. Pretty please. With sugar on top."

"Well, okay," I said, "only we're almost out of sugar."

"I know," said Daddy. "Soon as I get paid I'll do the shopping."

"Can I come?" I asked and he said Sure. I went to help Wendell so Daddy would know I understood the value of cooperation. I fished out the sponge and wrung the water into the sink, saving more than enough toilet water to sprinkle my brother but good. "Holy water," I said. "Maybe now you won't go to hell."

Wendell tried to spit out the experience and some of it got me in the chin. "Maybe now you will," he said with an evil smirk. He stuck out his tongue.

I sprinkled it with a fistful of holy water before making the sign of the cross. Wendell kicked my leg. I kicked him back twice as hard.

Since Mama had died, Wendell had been simply incorrigible. Daddy said to give him more time. Daddy said I didn't need any time and that was a compliment. Even though Daddy didn't play favorites, it was obvious he liked me best. For good reasons.

The experiments were the most important thing in Daddy's life right now. He tried to pretend it was all just a hobby, but I knew better. I understood exactly how Daddy felt. The experiments were the most important thing in my life, too. Daddy knew how to keep a person alive after death.

Not the whole person, because that was impossible and besides, it wasn't important. Because, what exactly was a person when you thought about it? I mean, really? When you thought about it, weren't we all just bunch of cells clumped together in slightly different ways that made us unique?

"All right, Lola," Daddy said. "We're ready for you now."

My legs turned cold and wobbly. I could hardly walk. This was the first tumor to live for so long outside of the host.

"A new breed," Daddy said, smiling like he had won a prize. "Not quite the person who died, but something that could live forever, could forever divide and grow."

The tumor was the size of a sour plum. Daddy had moved it from the Petri dish into a resealable sandwich bag with a label marked #403. The tumor looked like shiny pink coral, only with tiny veins like a freeway map. Something gray was puddled underneath.

Daddy handed me a rubber glove but I said, "No!" because I wanted to touch it with my fingers.

"Oh, honey," Daddy said, shaking his head. "It's too fragile! You could hurt the tumor, or else maybe it will hurt you."

"No tumor can hurt me," I said. "Mama wouldn't do that." I protested hard, but ended up having to pull on gloves before he'd let me get near. He was always so worried about germs and other things you couldn't see.

I opened the bag. With Daddy watching my every move I reached inside and stroked the tumor, delicately, like I was touching a butterfly wing and didn't want to rub off any color. The tumor pulsed. Liquid squirted from its bottom. "Look!" I said. "It's hungry."

Wendell tried to distract me by making rude fart noises from the corner. There were more important matters to deal with.

The tumor pulsed again.

"It likes you," Daddy whispered so Wendell couldn't hear.

I didn't want to be conceited—Mama used to say that humility came from angels while conceit came from the devil—but I was glad the tumor liked me better than Wendell. Glad enough it made my face warm. I blew it a kiss.

Daddy handed me an eyedropper and a bottle filled with clear liquid. He hovered over me like he was a yellow jacket and watched me feed it amino acids. "Slowly," he said. "Slowly."

It seemed like the tumor was growing before my eyes, bigger and pinker and more alive until it was pulsing, a tiny pale heart.

"She's so beautiful!" I said.

Daddy started to tremble. I put down the eyedropper and covered up the tumor and set the bag down on the counter. I took off my gloves so I could wrap my arms around his waist.

Daddy said, "Let's not get our hopes up."

"There, there," I said to comfort him. "Don't worry, Daddy. Can't you tell? She's going to live!"

Daddy got a faraway look in his eyes. "These little critters never asked to be brought into the world, but once they're here, well, we've got some responsibility, don't you think? They shouldn't just be thrown down the incinerator like garbage! They have as much a right to life as any of us."

"Of course, Daddy."

I looked toward the jar with Mama's tumor, pickled and okra slimy. He had rescued that tumor from the incinerator, brought it home and kept it alive in our laboratory. I wished Daddy had perfected his experiments in time to keep more of her alive, but it was too late for wishing, and we knew that. Except for Wendell.

Daddy took off his gloves and patted me between the shoulders. "Life is so... unfair. You can't change the past, only influence the future. Just don't look back." He'd been telling us that for a couple of months, only now—for the first time—I understood.

As I glanced back at Mama's tumor something wiggled in my stomach or maybe it was my heart. "Sorry, Mama," I whispered. Not that the thing in the jar was really my Mama. Bit it was alive. Mama was dead. Maybe, just maybe it was time to move on. Mama would have wanted it this way.

I hugged Daddy tight enough that Wendell couldn't squeeze in, no matter how hard he tried.

"She's alive," I said. The tumor was growing stronger by the hour. "I'm so proud of you!" I said.

Daddy hardly ever smiled, but he was smiling now. "I did it," he said. "The experiment is a success."

Lolerium.

"Well," said Daddy, pulling away. "Better put this lady to bed." He wiped his eyes with a grimy towel. He opened the refrigerator door, took out a beer and another Petri dish.

I wanted to dance, and grabbed Daddy's hands and tried to twirl him around the room. We had shared something big, something important. Wendell could never understand, he was too ignorant.

Daddy went along with me for a minute before saying, "Stop, Lola! I'm dizzy."

Sure, there were times I wanted our lives the way they used to be, before Mama got sick and Daddy got strange. Daddy wanted that, too—he just didn't know how to get it. But now that I was moving on I felt happy, really happy. I knew now what it felt like to be a mother.

I looked straight up at Daddy's face and gave him my version of Bambi-eyes. "Can I sleep with her tonight?" I asked. "I'll take good care of her. I promise. I'll keep her warm and safe and feed her and keep her clean. You said yourself, I'm very mature."

He was so full of pride he could hardly contain it. Daddy clapped me on the back and said in a voice larger than the world, "Sure! That will be fine."

I started to laugh like I had just heard the funniest joke in the world.

Wendell watched me, scared, and for good reason. When he woke up in the morning he was gonna be alone, all alone. So, Mama had loved him best, so what? She was deader than a wingless fly frozen inside an ice cube and there was nothing nobody could do about that.

Not the doctors. Not Daddy. Not me. Not my hopeless little brother. Wendell was just gonna have to get on with his life. The way that I had.

ALL MY CHILDREN

First appeared in *Women Writing SF as Men*,
Daw, 2003

When I was eighteen, I earned fifty dollars for ejaculating into plastic bags. It seemed like easy money at the time. I was a varsity wrestling star, president of the local chapter of the National Honor Society, school valedictorian, and a certified stud. I was also, arguably, an idiot. An Aryan-looking recruiter had bribed me with cash, fed me grilled double-cheeseburgers, and let me watch real porn movies. He'd promised the whole thing was legit—was I supposed to say no? At the time, it seemed like no big deal.

Segue to the future, when it was a big deal because I'd recently been informed that I'd fathered some 10,000 children. This came as something of a shock – to me, my wife, and our sixteen-year old twins (fraternal, neither of whom looked like me).

At the moment, my nuclear family and I were driving to the Rose Garden Arena, where my newly outed offspring were gathering for a reunion. It was not exactly a reunion, since none of us had ever met, but that was how they had billed it for TV. Officially, in the lawsuit, I was known as "The Donor," though my TV show was being called, "Life Without Father," which the producers thought had more appeal.

I was forty-nine, a surgeon in a thriving private practice, a Democrat with a house in the country, and a well-trained bulldog named Mr. Sniffles. I was a stocky blond guy with bifocals, a goatee, and a penchant for wearing tweed suits in public.

Circumstances had compelled me to forsake my tweed and get into something less comfortable. After suffering multiple fractures while skiing, I'd been immobilized inside a heavy plaster body cast that started at my neck and stretched to my waist and resembled a solid tee shirt. The plaster covered my shoulders but stopped above my elbows. It held out my upper arms to the sides scarecrow style, allowing my forearms to dangle loose. For this TV special, my wife Gina had draped a white dress shirt over my shoulders, and I wore new jersey pants with a drawstring waistband. A zipper was beyond my current means.

I was feeling a little tense, maybe because I was propped up on the passenger side of the Suburban without a seat belt, maybe because my wife was in the back seat pretending to be asleep, maybe because the boy was stoned and hiding behind earphones in the cargo hold, maybe because the only one in my family who was still talking to me was my daughter, who was doing ninety in a sixty-five mile zone and lecturing me about child abandonment and its role in the development of criminal behavior. I'd taken two codeine tablets, but they were hardly touching the pain.

"Eighty percent of the women in jail were abused as children," my daughter Letty said. "And a lot of them grew up in single parent homes without a genetically related male to protect them."

"You're not blaming me for everyone who's ever been in prison," I said.

"It's not like he was around for us, either," said Henry Junior said.

"True," Letty said.

I was tired of this complaint. "I'm a surgeon. It's a demanding job. I've been home every night except when I was on-call," I said. "You have the luxury of a portable CD player because I worked to give it to you."

"Okay, so you're 'Father of the Year.'" Letty had inherited her mother's dark hair and sharp tongue, but none of my athletic prowess. She was tall and slender, a sophomore who hoped to become a sociologist. I couldn't have been prouder.

Henry was a bit more complicated. He had his Neanderthal ancestor's stoop, not to mention personal hygiene habits, and had no interest in anything academic; for the past few months, Henry's life had revolved around drugs and rap music. Lately, every time we tried to talk, we ended up yelling. Which didn't mean I loved him any less, just that I worried more.

"Slow down," I said to Letty.

She ignored me.

"I can't believe I have ten-thousand siblings," Letty said. "What am I supposed to tell my friends?" She gave me buttocks eyes: a scrunched up angry expressed that showed how much she wanted to hit me.

"Look, I feel terrible," I said. How many times in one day was a man supposed to say he was sorry?

"I hate to be the saltshaker," said my wife Gina, coming out of her faux-coma, "but you're lucky *if* you only have ten-thousand siblings. There could be millions, you know. Millions! Think about it."

Letty squealed, "Eueweeuee! Do you *have* to remind me? Damn you, Father," she said, in her special teen sheep dialect that made it sound like "Faaahhhaahha-thur!"

I felt like I had lost leverage with the kids.

"Couldn't you have controlled yourself?" Letty asked.

"Well, no," I said. I was eighteen. "But I didn't know this would happen," I said. "I thought I was beating off for science."

"Oh, please," screamed Henry Junior. "Not in front of the children."

He was close to the age I had been when I'd fathered my first litter. This wasn't the kind of conversation I had expected to have about sex and responsibility. On the other hand, now it was sort of over and done, and maybe we could move on.

I saw the green sign that said, "Rose Garden Arena, next right," and tried to let Letty know to get over.

She screamed, "I know how to drive—you're the one who's a

menace to society," so I shut up.

Letty cut through three lanes of traffic to squeeze between a Greyhound bus and a gasoline tanker. I went sliding across my seat. As my elbow hit the window, painful shockwaves pulsed throughout my body. The combination of the codeine and teenage driving made my stomach vault and I felt like I was gonna be sick.

Letty made a hard right into the parking lot and almost ran down the guy directing traffic. She unrolled her window and dug through her pocket for the five bucks.

"Excuse me," I called past her to the boy in the orange vest. "We're supposed to have a place in 'Reserved Parking'. I don't think I should have to pay."

Letty glared at me and tried to shove a bill into the attendant's hands, but it was too late.

The boy's face lit up. "You're the guy!" he said. "You're the father!" He called over a few of his buddies and one asked for my autograph. "Does anyone have paper?" the first boy asked. Of course, nobody did, so he tore a parking voucher and turned it over and pointed to the blank spot and said, "There!" He thrust it through the open window, past Letty's nose.

If I tilted my body about forty-five degrees and wedged my head near the stick shift, I could just manage to scrawl illegibly with my right hand. "Sorry to ask this of you," I said to Letty, "but I need help."

Letty held the paper while I signed.

It seemed there were no end to the awkward moments.

Another guy in an orange vest let us through a wall of parking cones and we followed a marked lane to the VIP section near the main entrance. Letty pulled into a space marked by a huge plastic-covered sign that read, "Reserved for Henry Murkson and Family."

"Now are you satisfied?" Letty asked.

The press were waiting like car salesmen on a slow day and approached en masse.

"Why didn't you just let me pay the five bucks?" Gina screamed. She blared her horn and the press backed away.

"OHMYGOD!" said Letty. "I don't want to be on TV or in the paper! I can't tell you how much I hate you right now!"

"There's no need," I said, feeling the love.

"Could this be any more embarrassing?" Gina said. She opened the back door and pulled her coat over her head to run for the entrance. Henry followed from the cargo hold, his head down, and his arms shielding his face.

As Letty got out, she pressed the auto-lock behind her and ran off.

"Hey," I called. "Hey!" Nobody had opened my car door and I couldn't reach the handle on my own. "Hey!" I banged my head against the window, feeling useless. A few minutes later, a young woman in an orange vest tapped on the glass and waited patiently while I maneuvered my cast until I was able to press the release button.

She opened the door and I spilled out.

She was in her late twenties, very tall, slender, and pretty. She smiled, and I found myself smiling back, flirting just a little, even though I knew that from the front, with my cast on, I looked like a cartoon character flattened by a steam roller.

"Excuse me," I said. "My lawyer was supposed to meet me here, in the lot. Have you seen him?" Appearing on the show had been his idea, because he thought a guy in a cast would play sympathetically to the audience.

"Dad?" she said with a hopeful tone. She gave me a firm hug.

"Ouch," I answered.

Dad.

The cloudy sky swirled like vanilla soft-serve in a blue bowl; I pulled away and leaned against the side of the Suburban, lowered my head, and threw up.

The girl waited for me to finish before wiping my mouth with a crumpled tissue with pink lipstick marks in the center. She produced a bottle of water from the chest pocket of her vest and poured a little in my mouth.

The water was warm, but I drank it anyway. She gazed into my eyes as she dribbled water into my mouth. She gave me more than I wanted, and some dribbled down my chin.

She capped the water, and put it back in her pocket.

I burped. I'd just been bottle-fed by my new daughter.

Of course, a photographer from the AP caught the moment in a flash, but my daughter shooed everyone else away. She put one hand on my back to guide me toward the entrance.

"So, you're one of them," I said. "Somehow, I thought I'd know." My feelings were complex. I tried to explain. "You're the first one I've met."

"Sorry," she said. "I should have introduced myself sooner."

"Life doesn't prepare you for these kinds of moments," I said, hoping to sound wise. "What's your name?"

"Heather," she said. "Don't laugh."

"Why should I laugh?"

"Everyone does," she said. "My parents are both women. Or maybe you don't remember the book, 'Heather has two Mommies.'"

"Oh," I said, pretending not to be shocked. "Lesbians." My face got hot. "I hope you've had a pleasant life," I said. I wanted to reach inside my pocket for my billfold but couldn't do it. "I have money," I said. "I could give you some." I looked around for someone unrelated whom I'd feel comfortable asking to dig through my pockets.

"I'm okay," she said. "You don't need to give me money. I'm in college. This is just a part-time job. I really don't want anything from you. I just wanted to meet you. You know, say hello."

"I'm glad to meet you," I said, a line I'd practiced in preparation for these occasions. "I'm glad that you're okay." I couldn't help but be curious and blurted out, "Are you, you know, a lesbian, too?" I asked.

"It doesn't work that way," she said, and I could see that I'd offended her. "You have a lot of weird ideas about sexuality," she said. "But what do you expect for a guy who spilled his seed in a plastic bag?" She snatched her hand from my back and walked quickly away.

I understood that I was to follow her into the stadium. "Sorry," I yelled. "Sorry!" I was in no position to lecture anyone about alternate lifestyles. "I was just curious," I said, too late. I had poisoned the relationship. Luckily for me, I still had a chance with the other 9,999.

Without anyone to insulate me from them, newscasters and reporters swarmed and pelted me with questions.

"How's it feel to have so many children?"

"If the lawsuits prevail, how will you provide child support?"

"What does your wife think about all those other women?"

"No comment," I said, as my lawyer had directed. Where was he anyway?

"Do you have any favorites or do you treat them all equally?"

"No comment," I said. "No comment."

At last, I made it inside, where a security guard in a red jacket whisked me off to the underground tunnels. A guy in pleated slacks and a merino wool cardigan walked up and gave me an air handshake. "I'm Bill Burke, one of the promoters," he said. "Glad you were able to come. Nervous?"

"Well, sure," I said.

"That's understandable. Anyone would be. Now let's get you to makeup."

"Where's my family?" I asked, and Bill said, "They're in the stands, in a private skybox. You can join them later, during the halftime."

"There's a halftime?" I asked.

"For fifty bucks a ticket, we need to give them something," he said. "These kinds of 'Real TV' shows are never predictable. You need to have something fun in case reality is a dud."

A makeup gal powdered my face with a puff and someone from wardrobe, who introduced himself as "Jim, the prop master," fretted over my white shirt and cast, shaking his head and saying, "This won't look good for the cameras! Too much glare. It could make his face go dark on screen."

"That might be okay," I said, but nobody believed that I was serious.

Jim brought out a red cape with black fringe and tied me into it.

"All I could find," he said.

I saw myself in the mirror and looked like Zorro with unbelievably broad shoulders.

"That's a very manly look," said Jim. "You stud, you!" He gave me a playful punch on the chin.

Bill and Jim led me through the dark catacombs. The tunnels shook a bit, as if there were cows stampeding above us.

"Sounds like a rough audience," said Bill. "Hope they don't eat you alive."

We walked up a flimsy staircase to backstage and I peeked through a sliver in the curtain. On the grass field sat thousands and thousands of spectators in folding chairs—my children? Thousands more sat up in the stands. I felt dizzy.

Jim looked me over. "You're a little hard to mike," he said. "I think we'll have to go for the floor mike."

"Have you used a floor microphone before?" Bill asked.

I nodded.

"Just don't get too close."

"I know," I said.

Jim took over the explanation. "A lot of people, they think it's like a blow job, but it's not. Keep your distance," he said. "It's very sensitive! Okay, so that part's like a blow job. While we're talking blow jobs, there's one other thing—just remember, six inches. Stand *six inches* away and you'll be fine."

Bill rolled his eyes and said, "Showbiz people," and went to talk to the technician at the soundboard.

Onstage, the host warmed up the crowd with his Ed Sullivan impersonation. "Ladies and gentlemen," he said. "We're here for a rilly big shoe. Paternity with a capital 'P'. Sperm donor uber alles. The ultimate non-custodial deadbeat dad! Put your hands together and let's welcome your father, and a legend in donor circles, Dr. Henry Murkson!"

There were a lot of boos and hisses, but also whistles and applause, and in a while, the applause grew loud enough to mask the booing.

Jim made a few final adjustments to my cape and gave me a gentle push forward. "Go get 'em, tiger!" he said. "Grrrrr!"

I walked onstage and stood six inches away from the mike. "Hey, kids," I said. I looked at the faces of those sitting in the folding chairs and tried to figure out if anyone looked familiar. There were children, teenagers, young adults, and older people who must have been their parents. Then my mouth went dry and I started trembling, and the speech I'd practiced left me. I had stage fright for the biggest performance of my life.

The Ed Sullivan guy ran back to the mike and turned it off. He whispered, "Don't focus on any one face; just pretend you're looking at everyone."

I did as he suggested. It helped a little.

He flipped on the mike. "Well, okay, then. Let me ask you a few things. Your sperm was sold to thousands of well-to-do couples, who were told that they were purchasing a genetic legacy capable of producing Ivy League and Fortune 500 children, yet you claim you weren't informed about this at the time of donation?"

"I was never informed, no."

"But you signed a waiver."

"I might have signed something. I probably thought it was a form so I could be paid."

"Excuse me for sounding skeptical," said the Ed guy. "But didn't you ever think about what might happen to your sperm?"

"How many eighteen-year old boys do?" I said.

"Any questions from the audience?"

Hands flew up like butterfly wings and ushers holding portable mikes flitted through the audience. I looked up into the stands and saw a row of glassed-in skyboxes atop center field. The faces were too far away to pinpoint, but maybe the kids were watching. This might be my best chance to explain myself.

The Ed guy said, "Let us know your first name, your age, and where you're from," and a young man in a wheelchair said, "Jeremy, fifteen, from Boca Raton, Florida. Are there any genetic flaws that it might help us to know about?"

I cleared my throat. I sensed he wanted to blame me for his condition. I wished I could have given him that. "Not that I'm aware of," I said. "Sorry."

Jim brought me out a glass of water and whispered, "You're doing great!"

"Next question," said the Ed guy.

"Shelina, thirty-one, from New Orleans," said a young black woman. "Do you want to have more of a role in our lives?"

"I'm not sure everyone would want that," I said.

"Another question," said the Ed guy.

"Renee, twenty, from Salt Lake City. If you lose the lawsuit, are you prepared to pay child support?"

"I don't think that I'll lose," I said. "It would be a terrible precedent for all donors. When you think about it, I'm a victim, too."

There was a wave of booing that made me lose my nerve.

"Liz, nineteen, from New York City. What's it like to wake up one morning and find out you've got thousands of kids. Do you love us?"

I blanked, not remembering if the lawyer had told me to say yes or no to this question. "Could you repeat that?" I asked; the guy with the portable mike had already moved on. Too late, I recovered and said, "I love my children," but my mike was dead and nobody heard me.

"Excuse us while we go to a commercial break," said the Ed guy.

75

Two armchairs were brought out onstage for the next segment I was introduced to a famous TV psychologist and famous TV lawyer who were regulars on the series. We made small talk while Jim brought out an extra chair and rearranged the furniture, leaving space to the side. He straightened my cape and fluffed the sides of my hair. "The camera loves you!" he said. "Just remember that!"

I whispered, "Have you seen my lawyer? He's supposed to be here!"

"He's a no show," said Jim. "It happens. Sorry."

I tried to sit but couldn't fit in my chair. Jim ran off and returned immediately with a beanbag chair. He helped me down. We went live. The Ed guy introduced us all and asked the famous psychologist, "So what's the harm of having a turkey baster for a father?"

"Well, first of all, he's not the father, he's the donor," she said. "It's important to remember that being a father is sociological, not just biological."

"In an ideal situation," said the famous lawyer.

"But the point is, that in this case, none of the birth mothers were misled as to the intent of the donor. They went to a clinic expecting to meet sperm and not man. None of the birth mothers held the expectation that this gentleman would help them change diapers, or play ball with the children. This was a financial transaction, not a societal one."

"Many of these innocent victims in the audience would disagree," said the famous lawyer.

The Ed guy brought out a woman named Audrey and introduced her as the mother of one of my children.

She shook the others' hands but just stared at me and said, "I thought you'd be taller."

The famous lawyer laughed and said, "You never get what you paid for, do you? I guess the lesson is, Caveat Emptor."

Audrey took the chair that had been meant for me. "And they said my kid would have blue eyes but they turned out brown," she said. "At least I didn't pay as much as most of them. I bought the sperm on eBay." She pulled out her billfold to show a picture of her kid—my son—John. She flashed it my way.

He didn't look anything like me.

"I don't know what I'd do if you tried to take him from me," said Audrey.

"I don't want to take him from you," I said. The Ed guy ran over with the floor mike and told me to repeat what I had said. I shook my head. "I can't believe all this is happening," I said. "It doesn't seem real."

"Oh, it's real," said the TV lawyer. "The claimants have all had their DNA tested. But how about your family? How do you know that your children are really yours?"

"There's no need to test for that," I said. I looked up into the skyboxes and hoped Henry Junior was listening. "My children are mine," I said. "Case closed."

"You're so smug," said the TV lawyer. "I suppose you think that the other 10,000 are illegitimate?"

Audrey stood up and screamed, "Did you call my son a bastard?"

The three got in a fistfight, which I knew was staged because I saw Audrey slip a red capsule in her mouth a few seconds before the psychologist pretended to hit her in the chops. She spit blood over everything and for once I was happy to be wearing a red cape.

There was another commercial break and the TV psychologist and TV lawyer and Audrey all shook hands and left the stage. The next section featured four of my offspring: two girls and two boys.

"You're not—any of you—going to hit me?" I asked. I couldn't cower properly, because of my cast.

The four of them denied any bad intent.

We came back live. "If you've just joined us, we're here with the man who spawned 10,000 kids," said the Ed guy. "Let's talk with some of them now." He introduced us to Theodore, Jessica,

Brittany, and Jared. None of them looked like me. With me in my beanbag chair and the kids in their armchairs, the perspective was wrong, and even the eleven-year-old seemed taller.

"What's it like growing up with a father who isn't your real father?" asked the Ed guy.

Young Theodore said, "My father is my real father," and if I could have moved my arms, I would have applauded.

Brittany said, "You always wonder who he is and why he abandoned you."

"I didn't abandon you," I said.

"But still, you always wonder," she answered.

Jared said, "It makes you think about how stuff you don't think matters, really does," and the Ed guy said, "That's deep, man."

Jessica said, "What I want to know is, was it worth the fifty dollars?"

"At the time, yes. Now, no," I said.

She looked as if she might cry. "I don't mean it like that," I said. "Your life has much more value than fifty dollars."

The Ed guy said, "Of course, if you divide up fifty by ten thousand..."

Jared said, "What will it be like for you when you meet your grandchildren?"

I gulped. Oh God. Not another reunion.

"Do you ever think about us?" Jessica asked. "What we've gone through?"

This time I was quick enough to say, "Sure."

The Ed guy said to me, "Is there anything you'd like to ask your children?"

I felt on the defensive; the only thing I could think to ask was "Are you glad that you're alive?" That must have been a good enough question, because we cut to a commercial.

And just like that, it was over. Jim helped me stand and led me from the stage. He whisked me through the underground to an elevator. "Wait!" I said. "What about my shirt?"

"Thanks for the reminder!" Jim said. He pulled off my cape and punched the button to close the elevator.

"My shirt!" I called. The elevator rose up to and the door automatically opened at my skybox.

Letty stood by the window, drinking a soda. She was talking with a teenager who could have been her cousin but was probably her sister. The girl looked a little like me.

"Hey, Father," Letty said, noticing me. "Come here and meet Irene."

I walked close.

"Where's your cape?" Letty asked. "Superdad." She and Irene began to laugh.

I ignored that. "How do you do?" I said. "I'm Henry Murkson. Am I your father?"

"Eweeuuee! Gross!" said Letty. "This is Irene! My friend from school!"

Someone poked me on the shoulder. "But you're *my* father," said a young woman I hadn't before noticed. She was short and dark and didn't look anything like me.

"Oh yeah, Father, this is my stepsister, Cecily," Letty said. "She's from Portland! Can you believe it! All these years we've lived so close and never known each other."

"I can't believe it," I said.

"It's probably a good thing. Cecily is, like, a genius. She got a full scholarship to Johns Hopkins. She's already invented an engine that runs on storm-water. I would have been jealous. You know, worried you'd compare us."

"Oh, like that ever happens," said Henry Junior. His eyes were cape red and I couldn't tell if he'd been crying or smoking. Probably smoking, because boys his age didn't cry.

"Hey, Henry," I said. "Want to introduce me to any of your brothers?"

"Why would I want to introduce any of them to *you*?" he asked, and stomped away.

I wished I knew how to make things right with him.

79

Gina sat at the private bar, nursing a martini. I joined her and asked, "Mind if I have a taste?"

"Get your own," she said, and signaled the bartender to pour me a drink.

He did, then slid the glass before me.

"Excuse me," I said. "May I have a straw?"

He set a couple of coffee stirrers in the glass and held them straight while I sucked up as much gin as I could get through the tubes.

"Sorry," he said, before I had finished. "I got other customers. You're on your own."

"Nice show," said Gina. "I hope you're proud."

I turned around to see Henry drinking a beer with one of the security guards.

Nothing in life had prepared me for raising teenagers.

"I don't know what to do about Henry Junior," I said. "I feel like he's just fading away before my eyes."

"Can't you see how much you've hurt him?" Gina said.

"Yeah," I said. "I can. I just don't know what to do."

"Well, it's a little late to show concern now," Gina said. She tossed down her martini. "Maybe if you'd had more time to watch him win his soccer games. Or go to that spelling bee." She pounded her glass on the bar. "Another," she said.

"But now is all I have," I said.

Gina sputtered, "Well, isn't that just too bad?"

I felt a hand against my back—Jim's. "Hey, doc," he said. "Found your shirt." He draped it over me.

"Thanks," I said.

He frowned and gave me a look of concern. "Something's wrong," he said. "I just know it. Buy me a drink and you can tell me all your troubles."

Why not? No one else was listening to me. I called over the bartender and Jim ordered a pink lady.

"I'm a failure as a father," I said. "My children hate me."

"They don't hate you," said Jim. "They just don't know how

to talk to you about love. Give them a break! They're teenagers! People are idiots at that age, which you, out of everyone, ought to know. You have to make the first move. Go ahead. Be a man, you studly thing, you."

He made me laugh, but I knew he was right.

I got up from the bar and strode across to the far side of the box. I looked back, and Jim gave me the thumbs up. I don't know why, but that small gesture gave me courage.

"Come here, Henry," I said to my boy. Henry approached but refused to meet my glance.

"Son," I said. "I love you more than I can say. You're utterly unique to me. You're my boy—maybe not my only son, but the only one I love."

I wanted more than anything to hug him, to make things okay, like it used to be, back in the days when I was capable of hugging my children—just the one in each arm. "Can't you understand that you're the only son I need?" I said. "The only son I've ever needed?" My voice broke and my nose started to run. I felt overwhelmed by feelings I had no name for. "Come here," I said. "Please."

"Oh, go on and give your dad a hug," said Jim, sneaking up behind us. "He could die tomorrow and you'd regret this the rest of your life. That happened to me. I lost my dad when I was twenty. You don't know how many times I've since wished I'd been there to say goodbye."

Jim shoved Henry Junior forward until we were barely touching at the chest. I felt the warmth from his body penetrate my cast.

"Henry, I'm so sorry," I said. "For everything. Please," I begged him. "Forgive me."

"Dad," Henry said and leaned in against me.

"Kodak moment," said Jim.

We hugged, sort of, Henry Junior's arms flat at his sides, mine in a plaster straightjacket, the two of us incapable of reaching around to hold the other near.

i REMEMBER MARTA

First appeared in *Lady Churchill's Rosebud Wristlet #9*

The doctor gave a perfunctory glance toward the questionable mole on James Speck's arm. He smiled and said in his reassuring doctorly voice, "This looks fine. I can cut it out if you like, but if it were me, I'd leave it alone. Now let's talk about what's really bothering you."

"It's very odd," James said. "My memory loss, I mean. I remember most of the things that happen..." He paused, unsure just how to explain his problem. James was a salesman who knew enough to modulate his voice to sound somewhere between embarrassed and proud. He told the doctor that, although he was certain he had slept with nearly every attractive woman at the company, he couldn't remember a thing about the sex, not the slightest steamy sensual detail. He couldn't remember the women—not their names, not their faces—either, which, at the moment, seemed secondary.

The doctor asked, "What other kinds of things are you forgetting?" and James said, "Nothing. I remember everything except the sex."

"I'm seeing this type of thing more and more often," said the doctor, looking bemused. "From the nature of the complaints, I'm beginning to suspect this type of selective memory loss could be an STD."

"An STD?"

"Sexually transmitted," said the doctor. "You would not believe how many patients I've treated recently, who forgot the good times and came in complaining of ennui."

For the first time since noticing his problem, James was worried. Despite the associated stigma, he wanted this to be VD, which was, he thought, for the most part curable. If it wasn't an STD but some new and frightening virus -- perhaps a heretofore undiscovered strain imported from the tropics -- there was no guarantee that what he had could be treated successfully.

The doctor crossed his arms and sneaked a glance at his watch.

James could only assume he had been consistent in his use of prophylactics as his dread of offspring overrode his dislike of condoms; he could not quite remember. "It's not fatal?" he asked. This was bad enough, but he was prepared for the need to worry more, if warranted.

"Anything is possible," said the doctor, promising to do a literature search and get back to him.

James took the rest of the day off and spent the next two hours at the gym and in and out of the sauna before going home to rest.

At eight, he showered, brushed his teeth, and got dressed. He wore brown pleated pants and a starched white shirt, pigskin shoes, and a matching smooth as tears pigskin jacket. He kept an extra toothbrush in the glove compartment of the Volvo. There was a party that night, and since he didn't like to chew in front of people, he picked up a sandwich to eat along the way, then brushed his teeth.

Traffic was light for a Friday evening. The BMW parked in the driveway hadn't left much room for his Volvo; its right tire was sure to leave its brand upon the lawn. Ah well. The grass would grow back, but James's shoes were pigskin and worth saving.

He checked his teeth in the rearview mirror one last time to answer the question a salesman always had to answer: How much would it take to get them to like me? Not much, he thought.

I'm in, for sure. He looked great. He grabbed his hostess gift, a moderately priced bottle of Napa Merlot, locked the car, and made his way up the path.

Someone other than his hostess answered the door. She was about twenty and presumably only blonde from the waist up, his guess from the artificial sparkle to her hair. He wasn't sure, but he thought she worked in distribution. Either that, or in marketing.

He smothered her small hand with his large ones and said, "How are you?" He tried to place where he knew her from. Had they gone out? A movie perhaps? God, he loved women, loved watching them, being near them, touching them, smelling them. He never meant to take advantage. He was certain he'd remember her if he'd bought her dinner because you didn't forget people once you spent enough money on them. At least, that was the theory.

Her breath smelled of cinnamon and wine and she was barefoot. He was too old for her, but usually that didn't matter. How much will it take to get her to like him? I'm attractive, he thought. Financially secure. Sensitive to her needs. Not to mention the big "A" — available.

Her toenails were a painted rainbow, each a different color. "Asshole," she said, slipping from his grasp. She turned back once to sneer at him and flip him off before disappearing into the hall.

This type of thing had been happening all too often lately. He closed his eyes and concentrated until the vaguest of memories formed: a frantic groping in darkness, a tongue lingering over the sweetness of a nipple. But whose nipple? And more important, whose tongue? This was all so insensitive and unlike him. He was a detail-oriented guy, one reason why he got along so well with women. They liked that sort of thing, the attention. There was obviously some sort of unpleasant history with this blonde that he couldn't remember. Whatever it was, he couldn't blame her for being angry. Who wouldn't be?

It was terrible—not remembering about the sex, like never getting sex at all—a modern day horror story! Even worse, so many women were able to dredge up details he could barely imagine. He had heard rumors about an impending harassment complaint; rumors that he was about to be transferred to a new territory. That was the worst thing about his line of work: you never stayed in one place long enough to call it home.

James closed the door himself and looked for a clean place on the rack to hang his coat. If you weren't careful, suede would not last more than a season; James loved the look and feel of it enough to put up with its ephemeral nature. He moved things around in order to park his jacket inside an unwrinkled silk coat. You could tell a lot about people from their coats: whether they owned cats or fox terriers, or whether they smoked, whether they parented small children with continuously moist and dirty fingers.

Potted plants propped open French doors leading from the hallway into a large living room. The plants, braided fichus trees, were decorated with silver garlands and tiny strands of blinking lights. It was almost like Christmas except that it was not quite Halloween. The house was huge, more than enough space for the company party. James gave a quick glance into the living room and when he didn't see anyone he wanted to talk with, decided to take his chances in the kitchen.

The kitchen was steamy and warm, with spicy mulled wine scenting the air. His hostess stood with her back against the wall. She was wearing a sleeveless dress and her legs were crossed at the knees. She was elegantly tall and looked sexy in black. James made his way toward her. "Pardon me," he said, and inserted himself into her conversation with another of her guests, a balding man from collections named Clark, who despite his state of decay, was not all that much older than James.

"Here," James said, presenting the wine. The Merlot was impressive without being too pretentious. He gazed at the woman's face, letting his appreciation show. Too bad she was married, not that he would necessarily hold that against her. "A little something to thank you for inviting me."

Her face reddened. "James," she whispered. "I didn't invite you. I had no choice. Why do you do this?" She set the bottle on the counter beside several opened ones just like it. "Will you excuse me?" she said, but didn't wait for an answer. She hurried down the hall and up the stairs.

Clark leaned close. "I heard about you two," he said in such a smarmy tone that James wanted to punch him. But his curiosity got the better of him. "What did you hear?" he asked.

Clark balled up his fist and playfully nudged him in the ribs. "You know. The seven-year itch. You're the guy who scratched it."

James smiled. "Don't believe all the gossip," he said.

Clark winked. "Her husband's the one who told me. He's going to file for divorce after the merger. If I were you, I'd watch my back."

James had been in sales most of his adult life. He willed the smile to stay frozen on his face. "Always," he said, and slipped away. His stomach twisted up like a macramé wall hanging. He told himself he was only passing through this party, only making an appearance because it was expected of him. He checked his watch. A few more minutes and he could leave.

A guy from receiving, Lenny, high-fived him and blocked his exit from the kitchen. "You're the man," Lenny said. "The man. Tell you what, any time you want, you go ahead and introduce me to one of your dissatisfied customers. Anytime."

James noted a gob of spinach dip stuck between Lenny's teeth.

"There are no dissatisfied customers," James said. "There are only bad salesmen."

"Lucky man," Lenny said. "Admit it! You've slept with every woman here! Nice work if you can get it."

"Now what kind of cad would kiss and tell?" James said. He dismissed Lenny with a firm handshake.

The head of Human Resources managed to corner him beside

the refrigerator. Loretta was a short woman with prematurely gray hair and a dress that could have doubled for a pillowcase. She was a religious nut, which James defined as anyone who went to church more than he did, which was never. She seemed excessively smug for being so drab.

"Having fun?" she asked. She reached for a tray filled with cheese puffs.

"This is terrific," he said. "Great party."

"Isn't it though?" she said. She gripped his arm below the elbow. "You behaving?"

She acted as if there was an awful lot of intimacy between them. He couldn't remember fucking her, but that didn't mean much anymore. Except that he couldn't imagine ever seeing anything in her. Unless it was a long time ago, when she was younger and when he was a lot more desperate. Or drunk. Such things happened, even to him.

"Can I ask you something personal," she said. "Do you remember if we've ever, you know, been close?" She looked as confused as he felt. "Because I have this guilty feeling—maybe I was drunk and made a pass at you—I can't quite remember."

"I'm sorry," he said. "I don't know what you're talking about." He smiled politely and excused himself to use the bathroom. There, he locked the door and hung his head over the sink. Thank God, if they'd fucked, at least she couldn't remember either. He could have laughed, it was all such an odd *what was the sound of one hand clapping* sort of thing. Instead, he worried. The whole thing was terrible! A man like Lenny would never understand. What difference did it make to get as much sex as you wanted when you couldn't remember it after?

He grew lightheaded, like he wasn't entirely there. He splashed water on his face. It took a few minutes before he was ready to rejoin the party.

An attractive middle-aged woman with violet eyes that *had* to be contact lenses was waiting on the other side of the door to take his place. "Oh," she said and looked away. "James. I guess I should have known you'd be here."

"How are you?" he said. Who are you? he thought.

She was buxom and smartly dressed in a silk pantsuit. She took a deep breath and slowly exhaled. She assumed the pinched expression of a woman trying her best not to say what she was thinking. "I want you to know that I don't really blame you," she said. "Well, not entirely."

Given time, he would remember her name. Mary or Margarite or Mariah or some other name that began with Mar. He didn't want to talk to her and hoped that didn't appear too heartless. "I'm sorry," he said, though he didn't know what for. "I have to go."

"Wait," she said. "I can't believe it meant nothing to you. Tell me that at least."

"I'm sorry," he said. He left her there and walked through the living room and onto the covered patio.

His boss was sitting alone. Dennis patted the empty chair beside him and said, "James! Just the one I've been wanting to talk to." Dennis was queer and only liked him as a friend.

A waiter making his rounds stopped to offer a tray with glasses and a bottle of Merlot.

"Sir?" asked the waiter.

James nodded and watched the waiter pour.

The wine was smooth as Cool Whip, with less of an aftertaste. One glass was barely enough to calm.

"How are things?" Dennis asked.

"Couldn't be better," James said. Suddenly, he remembered her name, the woman with the violet eyes. Marta.

Dennis had been drinking, quite a bit from the looks of it. "You're a lot like my lover, Barry," he said conspiratorially. "The both of you switch sexual partners the way most people switch long-distance carriers. Funny, he doesn't remember any of them afterwards, either."

James smiled pleasantly while admitting nothing.

"I like you, James, but I don't know how much longer I can

keep you on," Dennis said. "We have to work with these women every day. This has got to stop."

How much would it take to make Dennis leave him alone? "I hear you," James said. "I promise to be more careful."

"Damn, you're one of our best producers," said Dennis. "I'd hate to lose you." He didn't sound entirely convinced. "It's gotta change," Dennis said. It was obvious he wanted to talk. "Sex is meaningless for you," Dennis said. "I just don't understand it." His eyes were bloodshot.

James disliked when men confided in him.

"Meaningless sex has a bad rep I don't think it quite deserves," James said with an air of smugness he didn't bother to mask.

Dennis didn't get the joke. "I bet you can't even remember everyone you've fucked!"

"And I suppose you can?" James asked.

"I've been with Barry almost four years," Dennis said. "When you have that kind of commitment it means something. I'll never forget the first time."

"And what about the twelfth time?" James said. "Can you still remember that?"

"Of course," Dennis stammered. His face was smooth as an ice cube and James knew he was lying.

Having won the argument, James stood.

For him, the party was over. He was just about to escape when he noticed a freckled redhead with full lips and thick glasses who seemed terribly uncomfortable and shy. Because he had never seen her before, he was certain she was new to the company. She wasn't bad looking; it was just that she hadn't taken the time to look good. Yet, something about shy women intrigued him.

"How do you do," he said, taking her hand. "I'm James Speck. From Sales."

"I'm Patricia Wirth, the new comptroller."

"When did you start work?" he asked.

"Just today," she said. She cleared her throat.

Nervous women always calmed him down. "You have family

nearby?" he asked.

"No," she said. "Just came out from Colorado for the job."

James was a natural salesman. When people asked his secret, he always answered that he tried to act respectfully around every customer he met. People liked that sort of attentiveness; it made them feel important, which they were. Everyone was a potential customer, he always said. Because you never knew how things were going to play out.

Patricia seemed relieved to have someone interested in being with her. She was lonesome; he could almost taste it. They chatted for another fifteen minutes, mostly her talking and him listening. He recognized that moment when she started to relax, when she stopped fidgeting.

He patted her hand and left to get her a glass of wine and a something to eat.

As he was filling a plate of sandwiches, Marta approached the catering table. She glared at him. He remembered something now about an unwanted pregnancy. Unwanted for him, maybe less so for her. But that was all water under the bridge now. How unfair that he did not remember the passion, only the discomfort. This disease of his acted as if a scorned woman had designed it. He hurried away before Marta tried to speak to him. "Here," he said to Patricia. "I hope you like blue cheese."

He looked back, growing increasingly irritated by Marta's sad expression. He didn't believe in children, not that they existed, just in the having of them. Children, family. Anchors that weighed you down when what you needed was to float free. He couldn't wait to leave this party. If he played his cards right, Patricia would leave with him. He wanted that as much as he had ever wanted anything.

"How do you like our warm weather?" he asked her.

Patricia said, "Does it ever get cold here?"

"Sometimes," he said. "But not for a while."

How much would it take to make her like him? Not much more. She was primed for the pitch. He let her finish her wine.

"I'm not much for small talk," he said.

"Me either," Patricia agreed.

"Even when I'm in a huge group of people, there are times when I feel so alone," he said. This much was true—there must always be an element of truth or you didn't make the sale. "It's very rare to find someone you have so much in common with."

They exchanged significant glances.

"I'm sorry for staring," he said. "You have a sexy smile."

She blushed.

They chatted another few minutes, about loneliness and feeling out of place. They moved on to the deep stuff: the need for something more, beyond living for the moment.

"I don't suppose you'd like to get out of here, go for a drive somewhere and really talk?"

"Sure," she said.

They retrieved their coats from the hall and he helped her into hers. His hand lingered on her back. On the front porch he slid one hand beneath her shirt and around to her stomach until he was touching the soft warmth of her breast. He kissed her neck and turned her around to face him. She smelled delicious, like far-away mountains. He pulled her sweet tongue gently into his mouth. Her ass was firm, round. He ground his pelvis against her, pressed an ear to her neck, and listened to the quickening of her heart.

She loosened his belt and practically ripped out his zipper and slid her soft hands beneath the elastic of his shorts and down, and down, as one grasped his cock and the other deliciously tickled his balls.

"It's too late for anyone else to arrive and too early for anyone else to leave," she said, breathless. She licked her lips and opened her mouth enough for him to see her tongue and imagine it licking him. "Where's your car?" she asked.

"Close," he said, just not quite close enough.

For the moment, he felt utterly grounded, secure, and alive. The uncertainty of the world no longer mattered. The pleasant ache in his groin radiated down through his thighs, electric, tingling, and erotic. He could barely stand straight, yet felt as if he could run and leap through hoops. No one could steal this moment of bliss and content. "Let's go," he said, breathless.

"Fine," she said, and in that heartbeat, he detected a subtle note of boredom.

"Where to?" he said, a courtesy.

"Does it matter?" she asked and led him away.

LOVE ME

First appeared in *The Infinite Matrix*
June, 2004

My wife, who is from Russia, and I are about to celebrate our tenth anniversary. Maybe celebrate is too strong a word for what we're doing. Observe might be a better choice, even commemorate, given the circumstances. I sit alone in her apartment, a bottle of California champagne on ice. it isn't real Champagne, like everything. Yelena will be home late; I heard she goes out dancing Friday nights. I can wait, after all, I waited until I was forty to get married. I am good at waiting. Plus, she has cable. It's weird how I can change the channels from my head using my brain implant. The implant doesn't work how it's supposed to, but does change the channels. I think it's defective. That would explain a lot.

Yesterday, I got a letter from a lawyer, explaining that the former Yelena Chekhov wanted a divorce. I'd sure like to hear that coming from Yelena; then I'd believe it. The problem, the same one we've had all along, is our language barrier. Yelena never learned English and I never learned Russian. We communicated by Charades until the implants that were supposed to change everything.

I'm not saying I'm the perfect husband, but Yelena is not an easy woman to please. In that way she's like most American women, not that I would ever have considered marrying one. They expect so much a man can never measure up. Yelena, on the other hand, expected nothing. That sure changed once she got here. I remember that first day like it was half an hour ago. She walks outside alone, showing off her new gold chains. Gets mugged her first full day in our country. She goes ballistic, refuses to leave the house again until I buy her a little gun, send her to a self-defense class taught by lesbians. I help her mom, sisters, aunts and uncles come over so she'll have her family. Takes a while, but her confidence returns.

Then we learn she's barren. She's heartbroken. We can't adopt—I'm too old for any agency. We can't afford private. I let her take a job as a social worker for Russian immigrants, and that keeps her happy and busy for a time. You never saw so many impoverished babushkas, coming to my house, eating my food, drinking up the Stoli. When they'd leave so would the clock radio, or my new bowling shoes gone and in their place a pair of mismatched slippers.

"Yelena," says I. "These people eat me out of house and home." She doesn't understand a word. My savings drop to zero. We take in a boarder named Mike to help pay the mortgage. He recommends a Russian marriage counselor, Dr. Nystroya, a quack who couldn't help Mike sort out problems with *his* Russian wife. I should have known.

Nystroya's office is above a Russian deli where Yelena likes the borscht. Our first appointment, we walk upstairs to ring the bell. A dark, disheveled man with eighties shag-rug hair unlocks the door, says something Russian, makes us wait in the hall until he changes into a yellowed lab coat and hustles us inside. I cannot understand a single word Nystroya says and I doubt he understands me. He has us sign papers for the implant, which I assume is routine. Yelena smiles. For one moment, I hope things will work out.

Next thing I know, Nystroya is shooting me full of drugs; a nurse with facial hair is shaving my head. Everything goes dark. I wake up. I'm given an instruction manual, written in Russian. "But I don't speak Russian," I say, and the nurse tries to tell me something in Charades. I figure out the pamphlet is the FAQ for the universal translator Nystroya has sewn into my brain. The device is supposed to translate my thoughts into Russian thoughts, translate Yelena's Russian thoughts into English thoughts. We should be able to communicate with the blink of an eye. If there's a disclaimer, I can't read it; the Russian manual is Greek to me.

Yelena points to the FAQ list. She blinks, three times hard and fast, and I stare into her eyes and try to interpret her thoughts. "A union waits, frozen in hellish Siberia" is as close as I get. I suspect there's something missing.

I blink three times, just like she did, ask, "What's for dinner?"

Her answer is to roll the FAQ into a tube and swat me on the side of the head.

I try again, "Honey," I say. "Let's go home. I'm hungry." Then I get wise to what she's saying. "If you'd rather not cook, we can grab a bowl of borscht downstairs."

Her words come so fast and furious that no machine can decipher them. I've said something wrong. Or maybe the device has made a mess of the translation. I'll never know for sure. Yelena heads for Nystroya's front door. I follow her out. In the morning, I wake up, knock on her bedroom door. "Did you make breakfast?" I ask, not because I want her to, but just so's I won't duplicate her efforts.

"You bacon!" she says.

"We have bacon?" I ask. She doesn't do the shopping anymore. She doesn't do anything. She's turned out really different from the woman I fell in love with from the mail-order bride brochure.

"Stuff the turkey," she says.

I figure she's confused, because Thanksgiving isn't for another few weeks. We keep trying to get along, at least I do, another few months. Things get worse. I can't tell if Yelena understands me, but I sure as heck don't understand her. The universal translator doesn't help. I start to doubt she loves me. Maybe she's a lesbian. That would explain things. Finally, she packs her bags, leaves. I hire a PI and track her down. She won't return my calls. The bank repossess my car. I have to give up cable. And now the letter from her lawyer. I'm so sick over the whole thing I can't eat. I can't sleep. My hair falls out in patches. My boss fired me a week ago. It's this device: it doesn't work. I have to explain to her, tell her I still love her and we should start over.

So I wait. And wait. Until I can't wait anymore. I polish off the champagne, real or not, and fall asleep. Boy, do I ever conk out. I must not hear Yelena come in, must not hear her gasp to see me sitting on her couch. Maybe she doesn't recognize me. I've lost twenty pounds and haven't shaved in a week. "You've come home," I say, lifting the empty bottle while I try to think up a toast.

Something's wrong. She's screaming. All this trouble I've gone through on her account and she still doesn't understand me. I wave the bottle around, trying to get her to calm down and find myself staring down the nostrils of a pearl-handled pistol. It looks like a toy. I start to laugh because I bought that gun out of love. "You wanna play?" I ask, thinking this is another game, like Charades, only with bullets instead of words.

She's serious, aiming right at my head. I sober up quick. I blink, five times, hard. "Don't shoot," I say, but I can't tell if my message gets through, or if she understands me loud and clear and plans to pull the trigger anyway.

THE MUTABLE BORDERS OF LOVE

first appeared in *Amazing Stories, #605*
November 2004

Though Marietta's eyes are closed, she is wide-awake, fingering the new sheets she gave Asher as part of his six-month anniversary present. The other parts were dinner, followed by multiple sexual favors. She has already thought ahead, to the seven-month anniversary, when she will trade dinner for breakfast, a languorous night of sex for a quickie. She worries to be thinking so far ahead, to have expectations about things she cannot fully control. Is this the way love is supposed to feel?

Asher's bed is a California King. It is out of place, too big for the eight-by-ten room. The sheets cost almost double the price of her queen-size, but she bought these for herself as much as him. Asher's new sheets are crisp and cool dense cotton that makes them feel shiny. Marietta is obsessed by their smooth texture, the fine weave. She can't stop fidgeting with the fabric between her forefinger and thumb. The old sheets were a remnant from a previous relationship. No matter how many times they were laundered, the Hawaiian ginger scent favored by the woman Marietta has replaced lingered like old smoke. Marietta hated sleeping over, until tonight.

Asher snores contentedly beside her, something she calculates will continue another ten minutes before he fades into a deep and heavy sleep, at which time he might call out names of women he dated before she met him. Marietta knows these women are all dead, just as her past sweethearts have all died, but it bothers her all the same, maybe because it's an unwelcome reminder that not everyone is strong enough to survive love.

In most relationships, someone wins and someone loses. Marietta has been fortunate, so far, to have won them all. She gazes over at the lump in the bed that is Asher. He has been fortunate, too. They are successful competitors in the contest of love. She isn't jealous, just insecure. Is love ever worth the risk? So far, for both of them, the answer has been no.

Street lamplight filters through the shaded windows of his apartment. In the dim light, the delicate pastel blue of the sheets dulls to computer gray. Outside, the wind rattles branches and pushes cool air through cracks in the window frames. Go to sleep, she tells herself, sweet dreams. It takes every effort to keep her eyes shut and lie motionless. She's waiting for what seems inevitable, for a ghost to appear as he has nearly every night for the past few weeks.

Her ghost's name is Lenny; he was her first lover. They were eighteen—late for her, early for him. If she were honest, she would admit that she used him, that she saw him as a means to an end. She was anxious to get it over with, to cede her virginity to her past. It wasn't until long after that she realized Lenny viewed her deflowering with more gravity.

Asher murmurs something in his sleep, a name perhaps, but not one that she recognizes. Asher is dark-skinned and dark-haired, stocky enough to spill over onto her side of the bed. The California King is oversized, and he's used to taking up more than his share. She doesn't mind. Lying beside him is oddly comforting, given that he has passed out and she is fretting. They are both naked; the warmth from their bodies forms a placid layer that stays trapped between the sheets.

The weather has changed to those days just before fall, the only time of year an apartment feels comfortable without either heat or air conditioning. It is man-messy here, with a ring around the toilet bowl, no counter space, and a yeasty aroma leeching from bags filled with beer bottles, bottles unsuccessfully hidden in the closet, awaiting redemption. Asher doesn't leave much room for her to fit into his life. In this way they're well suited. She doesn't understand women who sacrifice their independence for their men. Women like that die young. Asher's apartment reminds her of a foreign country, one she's welcome to visit, so long as her belongings fit inside a backpack.

"Go away," Asher says in his sleep.

A tickle of doubt crosses her mind that he might be thinking of her, but she tells herself that that's out of the question. They have been together long enough that she's certain she loves him, yet short enough that she worries things might fall apart, that one of them will move on, that their time together will be defined by memories and smells loitering in the furniture and bedding. Marietta is twenty-six and ready for this to be the real thing. She thinks Asher feels the same, especially since he is thirty-three, at that age where many men think it's now or never.

Her ghost, Lenny, is late. Maybe he's decided to respect the mutable borders of love and not show up, here, in her lover's bed, in the new sheets that mark a new beginning. The waiting makes her anxious. She's about to give up on sleep, slip into the other room to watch television, when she feels a slight sensation tugging at the covers just below her left foot. Her gut twists, relaxes. Her eyes flick open and adjust to the darkness. A ghost perches on the edge of the bed, staring at Asher. Marietta knows that it's a ghost because she can see through its lithe body to a cherry wood chest of drawers propped against the wall. Transparency is a ghostly quality she greatly admires. Mystical, yet honest. Intriguing. There is no human equivalent.

This is not her Lenny. This ghost is a woman she doesn't know, no doubt one of Asher's old lovers. The apparition looks to be in her early twenties, wearing a sheer negligee that's about as thick as a window screen. She sits as if posing for an art class, hands crossed at the knee, torso twisted slightly. She's a lovely thing, only the littlest bit scary because of her ghost-white hair, which is thin and patchy like the packaged spider webs sold at

Halloween. Her face is bathed in fluorescent green light and she's smiling, a beatific, disarming expression. Marietta isn't sure what to say to someone else's ghost. "Hi," she says at last. "You didn't wake me."

The ghost answers with a condescending look that conveys both boredom and disapproval at finding her ex-boyfriend in bed with another woman.

"This is awkward," Marietta whispers, because it's always better to acknowledge a problem instead of ignoring it. Obviously, this affair is over and Asher succeeded in moving on. Too bad about the woman, but these things happen when love doesn't go your way. Should she wake Asher? Or would that just make things worse?

The ghost shrugs. "He doesn't like to be awakened," she says.

"Can you read my thoughts?" asks Marietta.

"Sorry about that," says the ghost. "I forgot how that spooks y'all."

Keeping her mind blank takes concentration. Marietta is slightly afraid, an emotion only a step up from vague anxiety. "When did you two hook up?"

"Two-thousand two," says the ghost.

The answer provides relief because it's unlikely that the latest set of sheets belonged to this ghost. "Did you love him?" Marietta asks.

"More than you can understand. He really hurt me."

He must not have loved her much, Marietta thinks, or things would have worked out.

"I was better than you in bed," the ghost whispers.

It shouldn't, but this boast hurts and Marietta cannot keep from fretting that the ghost is speaking the truth. She pushes back her insecurity. "You're dead now," she retorts. "So how good could you be?"

"Don't underestimate me," says the ghost, rising from the bed. When she stands, her body extends from the floor nearly to the ceiling, elongated, like she is made of taffy.

THE MUTABLE BORDERS OF LOVE

Marietta hears primitive noises, growling and snorts. At first she thinks the sounds emanates from the ghost, but the growling moves closer, accompanying a change in the texture of the sheets. The fabric roughens from smooth water to broken glass. The growling and snorts are sound effects, a cheap parlor trick. Ghosts are good at effects, better than people. Marietta's arms itch—the more she scratches, the worse it gets—until hot, itchy bumps crop up through her skin. The temperature in the room rises; Marietta breaks into a sweat. Sandy granules cling to her skin.

"What do you want from me?" Marietta asks. She climbs from the bed, sweat dribbling down her face, temporarily blinding her. Her shoulders grow raw from scratching. Her skin burns. It itches behind her ears, between her thighs, inside her mouth. She can't stop raking herself with her nails. "This isn't fair," she protests. "Take it out on him. I didn't do anything to you."

"Good point." Ghosts enjoy showing off their powers. They're quite human in that respect. "Listen," the ghost says. "Sorry, things got out of hand. I just came to warn you. So you don't end up like me."

"Don't worry, " Marietta says. "I won't end up like you."

"There are worse things," the ghost says with a dismissive wave.

Marietta's skin dries and the itchy feeling passes as quickly as it began. She's annoyed. This ghost isn't from her past; she's from Asher's. Marietta shouldn't be responsible for his mistakes, as well as her own. As if on cue, Asher calls out in sleep, "Inez!"

"It's good to know he still thinks about me," says the ghost.

"No," says Marietta because Asher should be thinking of her. "It's just a dream."

"Yes, of course," says Inez. "I didn't mean to hurt you or get you so worked up."

"Is that an apology?" asks Marietta.

Inez laughs. "Sure," she says. "Sort of."

Marietta cracks a smile and senses some barrier breaking

between them. She trusts this ghost, senses she means well. "'Inez' is rather old-fashioned."

"It's a family name."

Family names seem like gloating. Marietta thinks of all the family lines she's ended by being the lone survivor. How sad. She's sorry to have been so inconsiderate.

"Asher is afraid of commitment. You two will have another week, two at most. He'll win, you know. Asher's very strong. He's never lost."

"Neither have I," says Marietta.

"You haven't played against Asher."

"It's not a game."

"Not exactly, no. But there's always a loser. Don't you worry that your luck will run out?"

Inez is right: rarely do both parties survive intact. But it can happen, if both want it enough. Maybe it's not the norm, but she knows of people who love for keeps. "Why are you telling me this?"

"It's complicated," says Inez.

"You're still angry."

"Not with you. Just with him. I can't forgive what he did to me."

"It won't happen to me," says Marietta. "I'm strong."

"That's what I used to say," says Inez. "By the time you understand it all, you're already dead."

"I'm fairly experienced," Marietta says.

"Experience doesn't help," says Inez.

"I asked you before: why are you telling me?"

"I don't want you to die," says Inez. "This might sound funny, but I've found someone else."

"Good to know there's love after death."

"The weird thing is you knew him. His name's Sheldon Perricone."

"I know him," says Marietta. She corrects herself. "Knew him." Good old Sheldon. Somewhere between Lenny and Asher.

It turns out that a man she abandoned on the altar has found love with Asher's old girlfriend. "Small world," says Marietta.

"Sheldon loves me, but I can't take a chance that he loves me more than you. Not just yet. If you die.... We need more time to make it work. That's why I want to warn you. I'm not being nice—just cautious."

Marietta nods. This makes sense, in a weird, metaphysical, lovesick sort of way.

"Promise you'll be careful. Asher is sneaky," says Inez.

"So am I."

Next, there's a loud yawn and a stirring as Asher lifts himself to a sitting position on his side of the bed. He rubs his eyes. "Are you talking to someone?" he asks.

They are alone.

Inez has vanished.

"What's the matter?" Asher asks.

Marietta snuggles beside him and wraps her long legs around his muscular ones. She kisses his neck, while he strokes her back. He's so warm, so dark and substantial, nothing like a ghost. Her body-warmth returns. "It was nothing," she says. "I couldn't sleep."

"I don't mind," he says, and she can feel him growing hard beneath her touch.

The next morning, while in her office catching up on email, Marietta gets an instant message from someone named SP. Caught off guard, she answers and soon finds herself corresponding with her old, dead boyfriend, Sheldon Perricone, the ghost who is now partnered with Inez.

<Marietta> So, do you have a fast connection up there?
<SP> LOL. How about you?"

She agonizes over what to say next, feeling both curiosity and dread at continuing the conversation. She's just about to type "I'm

103

okay," when her monitor goes dark and a voice from behind her says, "It's better if we talk in person. I was never a good typist."

And there is Sheldon Perricone, whom she had loved and left so long ago it seems like another life. She hadn't meant to be cruel. She never meant to be cruel. With any of them. Human interaction is not an exact science, so there's bound to be mistakes along the way.

Sheldon stands naked in the middle of a plant stand. Philodendron leaves surround his abdomen like a tutu. She sees straight through his chest, though his face seems more solid. His eyes, no longer an intense ocean blue shade, have dulled to gray, with milky quartz crystals as their centers. He's watching her, waiting.

"You're forgetting something," he says, and old memories wash over her. He had hinted of a plan to propose one morning and at night, instead of meeting him for dinner, she had gone out drinking, met someone new, enjoyed a very fun, very sexy one-night stand with a stranger. She remembers telling Sheldon it was over, remembers a face that grew angry, then despondent, remembers watching him fade away before her eyes. It was horrible. Her guilt has come and gone, but at the moment, the feeling pulses strong. "Sorry," she says. "I guess I wasn't very nice."

His expression is sorrowful and vast; she's first to break away from eye contact.

"Should I say more?" she asks.

"Mistakes were made. It won't help to talk about the past."

"I was young."

"Don't make excuses," Sheldon says. "I was young, too. I forgive you. Just don't make excuses."

She wills herself to be quiet, sensing that she seeks something from him, something she cannot fairly ask. She would like to be pardoned for all mistakes, not just those mistakes she made with Sheldon. She doesn't want to be a bad person. It's just that being a good one is too costly. Sheldon, for example. What did being good buy him? He lost. "You have to move on," she says. It's a vacuous statement, one she immediately regrets. "How have you been?" she asks, though the answer is obvious.

"You've met Inez, I hear," he says. "I love her very much. I think she's my soul mate."

Her jaw drops, and while she's tempted to contradict him, she cannot believe what he has said. Does true love only happen after you're dead?

"No," he says, reading her thoughts. "Not always. We find love where we can. I just wanted to warn you. Asher loves you. Don't mess up. Not everyone gets another chance."

She's recovered her cynicism. "Are you afraid I'll dump Asher? Is he that much of a threat?" she asks.

"You've got it all wrong," he says. "You're worrying about the wrong things." He disappears without so much as a subtle whoosh.

On the bus ride home from work a man across the aisle gives her a look that could be interpreted as simple friendliness, or could be interpreted as an invitation. Isn't he worried about what she'll do to him if she gets the chance? Is the urge to pair up so strong it would make a reasonable person risk his life? She has power over men, something they all recognize. It never stops them. It doesn't stop her, either. Everyone thinks they are in control of the situation.

The man stands up and moves across to sit beside her. "Hey," he says.

"Do you want to die?" she asks and flashes a look she hopes signifies contempt. She stares ahead, refusing to meet the stranger's glance.

She notices she's fidgeting. The ghosts of her past have unnerved her. She accidentally skips her stop and has to backtrack several blocks. Breaking up is hard to do, though she is better at it than most. But she really does love Asher. She's sure he loves her, though if she's wrong, it will be the end of one or the other. She wants more than anything to be right.

Later, she'll meet Asher at her place to watch Survivor, which now holds an especially ironic twist. She's running late enough there will barely be time to call for pizza, let alone shave and straighten up. No choice but to settle for a spit bath and quick rubdown with a towel. She has already picked out a silk shirt to match her jeans. The bell chimes, signaling Asher has arrived.

"Coming," she yells, wishing she'd had time to change her bedding. Her sheets are old and threadbare, a suddenly significant fact. She can't ignore all the ghosts who have slept beside her in her bed. Some part of them still lingers in her life. They get in her way, make it difficult for her to fully commit to love.

She sets her towel on the bed and pulls up her panties and jeans, dabs Must de Cartier perfume at her pulse points, and wonders if it's worth the effort to wear heels that will come off the second she sits on the couch. She picks up the shirt, no bra. The doorbell rings again.

From behind her, she hears conspiring whispers. She turns around. Lying on their backs, smoking cigarettes, pale and naked, are three gossamer men she once thought she loved: Lenny, Sheldon, and a one-night stand whose name is hidden just a bit lower than the tip of her tongue. The worn sheet covers the lumps of their genitals.

Terrific. Her ghosts have hard-ons.

"Hey there," says Lenny. When he exhales, his smoke has more substance than does he. He points to her shirt and moves his fingers in increasingly small circles. Her silk shirt flies up from her side and hangs fluttering in the air like a fabric kite.

"Come sit beside me," says Sheldon with a tap on the sheet. "Plenty of room," he says. "I could use some company." When he nudges the pillow his elbow passes straight through it.

"You were something," says the one-night stand. "But you said you'd call. Why didn't you call?"

They mean to scare her. But they are dead and she's alive. The scariest thing that could happen has already happened, to them.

"What do you want?" she asks. "It's over. I won." It sounds harsh when she says it straight out, yet true.

Her ghosts smile with hollow lips. They act as if they don't believe she's the victor.

Sheldon blows her a smoke kiss. "It's not over 'til it's over." The room grows ominously cold.

There's a knocking at the door. In the distance, Asher shouts her name. He's a punctual man who expects no less from the woman he dates.

She checks her watch. "This has been fun but I gotta go."

"Stay," says Lenny, his cold stare pricking like nettles.

She stands up, feeling shaky, says, "Go away!"

"Make us," says Sheldon.

They think she's to blame, but she didn't make up the rules. They knew what they were getting into when they hooked up with her. She tried to love them. It just wasn't meant to be. She wasn't ready. That's not the kind of thing you know until it happens. She snaps her towel and the specters disappear one by one, pop back up, and disappear again. Flustered, she throws her shoe. It passes through Lenny and bangs against the wall.

"Come back with us," says the one whose name she has forgotten.

"Too late," she says.

Lenny sniffles. "You sure know how to hurt a guy's feelings."

"Tell me something I don't know," she says and pulls the old sheet from the bed to wrap around her shoulders. She styles the sheet over her head and looks out at a room that is daytime foggy, with just enough light peeking through the blinds that her furniture looks like boxes. Her hands appear almost transparent. A creepy effect, but one that makes her laugh. Who says that being a ghost isn't fun? She rushes from the room, toward the front door.

She hears them rummaging through her things, hears their footsteps follow her into the living room. They make the lights dance and topple books from the shelves, but their efforts fall short. She's made up her mind to forget them. They can't touch her. "It's too late," she says. She says it again, louder. Shadows appear through the fabric of her sheet. The shadows lengthen and twist like jungle vines. She trips on something she cannot quite see and pitches forward. "You can't get me," she says. She's stronger than they are; she's stronger than any of them. She's proved that by surviving this long.

Still, her pulse races.

She anticipates what will happen when she opens the door. Asher will smile when she answers, when he sees his lovely, ghostly girl hidden beneath her sheet. He'll pull away the fabric, notice she isn't wearing a shirt. They'll make love on the carpet. Sex, when it's good, makes her forget about the problematic things, like love. She's afraid of love but with good reason. Loving can be dangerous. Is it really worth the risk? Fear is an icy river coursing through her veins. Fear is a dust devil in her throat that makes her cough and choke for air. Fear is the stabbing pain in the gut that comes from uncertainty. Marietta is afraid because she cannot know if it's worth the risk until too late.

The ghosts laugh and groan. Their voices strangle and then sputter out like a fire doused with sand. When she turns the ghosts are faint ripples. Their steps slow, come to a halt. Their rustling movements fade to silence. As suddenly as they appeared, their spirits vanish.

She's won again. It should feel good, but it doesn't.

Knocking.

Asher waits for her to let him in.

She can barely make out the frame of the door through the worn sheet. She stumbles forward, twists the lock open, pulls back the door. A dark form wavers on the other side of the threshold.

Relief floods through her as she recognizes him. She hesitates before speaking. "Hey," she says.

"Hey," he answers. Once he steps inside he winds his arms around her. The door closes softly behind him. "Missed you," he says. There's a slight warble to his voice, like he's worried. He holds her so tight it's difficult to breathe. He nuzzles her neck through the sheet, breathing in the sweet scent of her laundry soap, her spicy perfume, the salty fragrance of her skin. He's told her how much he adores these things. "I love you," he says. He waits for her response.

It would be easy to comfort him, to say that she loves him. It would be easy to lose herself in love. Because she does love him. And that terrifies her. She wants to tell him, but she can't make her mouth form the words. It's too dangerous to admit how she feels. She can't do it.

He brushes her lips with his.

She pulls away from his kiss. "I'm sorry," she says.

His arms stiffen. He lifts the sheet from her face and stares into her eyes. His complexion has the clarity of old bath water. His affect is flat. "Why?" he asks.

"Asher," she says. She doesn't want to explain. She leans her weight into him, pressing her breasts flat against his chest, unable to feel the thrum of his heartbeat through her skin. A slow chill trickles like a tear along her spine. "Sorry," she says. "I really tried."

"Congratulations. You won."

"I didn't think this would happen," she tells him, but that's not exactly true. She suspected it would end this way. It always does. She feels bereft, alone, empty. For the first time in her life, she understands love, how it is best defined by loss, by what is missing, not by the transience of joy.

"It hurts," Asher says.

She holds him tight, not to comfort him but more to hold her own feelings of regret. In the end, he slips through her grasp and floats upward, to a place where love has no boundaries, where it floats like the memory of artifacts trapped in amber.

"I love you," she says, too late for him to hear.

PAPER MATES

First appeared in *Asimov's*
June, 2001

Farkas waltzed into his lobby feeling more refreshed and alert than he had in years. He was not wearing a top hat or he would have tipped it toward Ernest, the security guard. He did not know how to dance or he would have kicked up his heels. But smiling came naturally, so Farkas wore a silly grin that made his cheeks ache.

He had spent the past two weeks scuba diving in Maui with a stunning redhead named Toni, whom he had met in the Hilton lobby. In a most amazing turn of events, when they parted, Toni had promised to call him every morning. He was in love, or at the very least, in lust.

"Looking good," said Ernest, the security guard.

"Feeling great," Farkas replied in a chipper voice that did not sound like his usual frantic self. He knew he looked good. The suit was casual beige linen and stylish. Seldom had he allowed himself a tan like the one he wore now—skin damage and all—but he had gone to the Maui, dammit, and if you couldn't get some sun in Hawaii, then what was the point? He jogged past Ernest and just managed to catch the elevator. At the eleventh floor, he pushed through the crowd and stepped out.

Farkas had gotten on at Bleecker & Zoop immediately after college. It was the perfect firm for a workaholic. Bleecker & Zoop encouraged their employees to put in overtime by providing fresh-ground coffee and chocolate-covered espresso beans at conveniently located snack stations throughout the office. They offered on-site childcare so that parents needn't waste time on transporting children to and fro. There were saunas and showers, and even pleasant sleeping rooms on the north side of the building.

Farkas walked down the hall toward his office.

"Morning," said his secretary. "Thanks for the postcard." Sarah was guillotine sharp and tremendously efficient. Her desk looked like a magazine ad, with everything in its place. She was like a mother to him, except she never made him pick up after himself or criticized his hair.

"It's been a madhouse," she said. "As usual. And, uh, there's something I should warn you about before you go inside."

He was distracted by thoughts of Toni and barely heard her. He opened the door and took a step forward. "Ohmygod!" he said.

Paper buried his desk and formed huge mounds like those made by African termites. His fax machine had erupted and left a flow of creamy white messages across the carpet. The answer machine blinked red and there were boxes and boxes of orders requiring his immediate attention. Paper clips lay scattered about like champagne corks. Farkas had expected that a little work would pile up, but this was ridiculous.

"Sarah!" he cried. "What's going on here?"

She hurried to stand at his side. "I'm sorry, Mr. Farkas. Things got a little weird here after you left."

"Ohmygod!" he repeated with a shudder. This looked like a hell of a lot more than two weeks' worth of work; it was almost as if his office was punishing him for deserting it!

"I'm sure it all looks worse than it really is," Sarah said. She backed away. "I'll just leave you alone."

Farkas started with the phone messages, and by lunchtime had managed to listen to most, even made a few callbacks. He buzzed Sarah on the intercom, and when she answered, he said, "Could you bring me back a sandwich? I don't think I want to take time to go out."

"Sure, boss," she said. "Tuna on rye or falafel?"

"Whatever you're having," he said. That was the least of his concerns. He might never get through all this paperwork! Never get home to hear Toni's smooth-as-chocolate-mousse-voice, and arrange for their next glorious rendezvous.

"I've just got to go make copies of something, then I'll go find lunch," Sarah said.

"Thanks," he said, downhearted but grateful for her assistance. He turned on his computer, in need of a little mindless work while reality settled in. There were a thousand new email messages to attend to; he deleted without reading the most obvious spam, and brought the number down to four hundred. In a little while, Sarah brought his lunch and he ate it in a daze, never noticing whether he was consuming canned tuna or fried garbanzos.

Farkas worked well into the night and managed to create a small clearing. At some point, he closed his eyes and fell asleep.

Around three, he heard something whispering, and slowly opened his eyes, but did not move. A paper clip whizzed by and bounced off his computer monitor, landing in his lap. When his eyes had adjusted to wakefulness, he saw the most horrendous sight imaginable.

An overdue bill and a spreadsheet were furtively pressing against each other in the corner of the room. Their crinkling and fluttering grew more furious with every passing second.

They were mating. That explained everything! There was no mystery as to what had happened in the last two weeks. While he was away screwing around in the tropics, his paperwork had been screwing around in his office. Even more disgusting, it had reproduced. Jeez! he thought. How did they keep from giving each other paper cuts?

Curiosity got the better of him, and instead of stopping the bill and spreadsheet in the act, he watched—with complex feelings of disgust and the need to compare—to see how long it would take them to do "it". Not long, which seemed a disappointment, until Bill, apparently the male, fell away from the spreadsheet and immediately jumped a profit and loss statement. Without missing a beat, the two were furiously humping away. The staple on the profit and loss statement popped off and flew across the room. Seconds later, Bill blew away and landed on top of a pile of junk mail catalogs.

Ohmygod! Farkas thought. He gazed around at the stacks of paperwork with newfound respect. One guy did all of this? The audacity made him smile with brotherly pride until the spreadsheet began to crumple then unfold. Farkas realized with a start that it was about to give birth.

"No!" he screamed, not caring that he had blown his cover.

The movement of the papers stopped once they were aware that he was watching.

He rushed over to the corner and grabbed the fecund spreadsheet, her ardent suitor and his newest object of affection with his thumb and forefinger. He held them all at arm's length. "You slut," he admonished the little fellow.

Bill hung limply without response.

Now what? He had to do something quick before there were more papers to plow through. He tried his best to recall everything his science teachers had ever said about reproduction in invertebrates or about the scientific method.

There had to be a reason that only work undone could multiply. Because once you took care of things, recycled or stored files neatly away in cabinets, you could practically forget about it.

Obviously, file cabinets were invented to be a morgue for paperwork. It made sense that paper required light in order to reproduce—the photocopier flashed a bright light and suddenly the paper population doubled.

Yes! he thought. Darkness held out a solution to the whole problem!

Farkas was getting a headache. None of this made any sense, and yet it did, but not in any normal kind of way. Just then, a postcard fell from the catalog and landed on the floor. "Sign up a friend to receive this free mailer." it said. Another postcard spiraled downward.

There was no time to waste. Farkas tested his darkness theory by setting Bill in an inter-office envelope marked FOR IMMEDIATE DISPOSITION. He filed the spreadsheet in the cabinet and set the catalog in the recycle bin. He waited anxiously with his eyes closed, terrified he'd fall asleep and papers would mate again and produce more work and then he'd have to take them to the paper shredder, something he'd just as soon not think about.

Nothing happened. His theory about paper reproduction was right.

Unfortunately, the fax and the answering machine had been at it again, so while he'd solved one problem, he hadn't made a dent in the others. He was afraid to look at his email. Spam reproduced like bacteria and there wasn't a thing anyone could do about it. He stared at the fax and reasoned that it had masturbated and spat out loads of paper on orgasm. As for the answering machine—God only knew how telephones did it, what with underground cable and all.

Then, inspiration came to him like a mouthful of hot sauce. He listened to his message on his machine.

"Hello, you've reached... blah blah blah...I'm not in...blah blah blah...but if you please... blah blah blah. On and on it droned. How was it that he'd never heard himself blather before? It took forty-five seconds before the beep, more than enough time for sex in another dimension. He needed to record something else, something simple and to the point.

"Leave a message," he said.

Beep.

Ohmygod! he thought. What about Toni? He glanced at his watch. If he hurried, he'd just make it home in time to catch this morning's call.

He stared at the fax machine. I've got it! he decided. Limit access and you limit production! He opened its belly and removed nearly all its paper.

Let it think before it faxed, the way everyone else did. Feeling smug and happy enough to kick up his heels, if only, etc. etc., he hurried out the door and made his way home.

Her call came just as he walked in. Without realizing what he was doing, Farkas was soon having phone sex with Toni.

Only later would he shudder at the memory.

In the next few weeks, it became all too apparent that Bleecker & Zoop did not appreciate him. Farkas had dutifully reported his findings to upper management, who didn't seem to give a fig about exploding paperwork.

So Farkas decided to go into business for himself and call the company Planned Paperwork. Sarah was only too happy to become his equal partner. The business was successful from Day One, and just announced its initial offering on the NASDAQ.

Toni managed to transfer to a corporate division close by. She and Farkas maintained their glorious relationship, screwing like spreadsheets every chance they got. In addition to the usual precautions, to keep from reproducing, Farkas took his time and always turned down the lights.

PiCTVRE A WORLD WHERE ALL MEN ARE NAMED HARRY

First appeared in *Quantum Speculative Fiction*,
issue 2, 1998

You arrive at the Dating Zone, a little later than intended, and go immediately to the dispenser for a number. Though it is almost noon, the number is only 49, meaning the counter has been reset—at least once—to zero. The room is full, yet oddly silent, with hushed whispers and screaming babies competing to be heard above the clatter of back office keyboards. You take your seat and glare at the sign above the front door reminding you Today is Your Lucky Day!

It would be nice if management had the sensitivity to change that message every few years instead of rubbing it in, but these days, sensitivity is considered gauche. A Dating Zone counselor would tell you without sympathy, "That's the way it is in the love industry. Seller's market. Deal with it. Next!"

Still, it would be nice.

Too bad someone doesn't take a gun to that sign, and while they're at it, put everyone in the office out of their misery. You feel guilty enough about your situation as it is. You're getting on in years and still haven't found love.

What if your mother was right? What if you don't deserve happiness? But maybe your mother, rest her soul, was wrong. Today is your lucky day, at least that's what the sign promises. In a while, the receptionist calls your number. You stand, take a deep

116

breath, and approach her with the hope that you don't look too anxious. She slides a clipboard holding several forms across the counter. Staff has thoughtfully attached a pencil with a string so short you can't chew the end of it while you mull over questions like, "Do you prefer a tall? A medium build? Do you like your Harrys in a jogging suit or dressed for work? What's the longest time period you've ever stayed with one Harry?"

You narrow down the choices, trying to be honest even when you know that makes you look bad. Maybe this time things will all work out, maybe the fortieth time will be a charm—it could happen—it's happened to people you've read about, people you know, your best friend, in fact. You hand back your answers and return to your seat to wait. And wait. And wait. There's a steady stream of counselors hurrying from their desks to the bathroom. They're pissing on company time—on your time really, since you indirectly pay the bills—and there's nothing you can do about it. You'd visit the bathroom yourself, but if you miss hearing your name called you'll have to re-schedule your appointment yet again and that's even more stressful than having to pee. You cross your legs and do your best to ignore the feeling of pressure. Self-control is always easier with enough motivation.

Round two, the lineup, is held in the small auditorium. You sit in a folding chair beside eleven others who share your predilection for big Harrys with dark hair and full beards. Handy, able to fix things. Smart, but not over-educated—two years of college. Everyone knows the type. A counselor takes orders for drinks. "Make mine a diet," you say. Several shoppers murmur in agreement.

Before you hangs a purple curtain, masking a one-way mirror. The MC, wearing a black sequined tee shirt under leather lederhosen (shiny shoes, no socks), stands on a platform. He grabs a mike from its stand and tosses it into the other hand. "Welcome to round two! May we now present our bevy of beefy boys! All Harrys. All the time. Choose yours today!"

If you were in a better mood you'd think about laughing.

The curtain opens as a light is switched on; the Harrys are posed, illuminated from above as if works of fine art. A group sigh rushes like water from your side of the window. The person to your left starts the questioning in a timid voice.

"Harry Number Nine...are you a lucky guy? And if I choose you will I be lucky?"

The Harry scratches his head. He's broken into a sweat and you can tell he's nervous, but trying not to show it. "Am I lucky?" he echoes. The counselors have taught all the Harrys this technique—called reflection—and they repeat every question in an attempt to make you believe they've understood you. "Am I lucky?" Harry asks again. "I suppose you could say I'm lucky just to be standing here." He smiles as if he's given the perfect answer. He's looking at himself in the mirror, though it is supposed to look like he's looking at you. He winks. The questioner giggles.

What a bunch of losers.

Someone from behind you calls, out of turn, "I'd like to ask Harry Number Twenty something." Then a little hemming and hawing before, "What do you think is the secret to a successful relationship?"

Harry number twenty doesn't pause to take a breath. "What is the secret to a successful relationship? Communication," he says, "respect, and maybe after that comes physical attraction."

This Harry is a few pickles shy of a jar.

It's your turn to ask the next question. You've been a little cautious since that last bad experience with that disgruntled postal worker, and want to take your time. You wish there were some better way of doing this, some more exact method, maybe even scientific. You want to make the right choice, whatever that is. You notice one guy staring at his feet, his lips pressed together like he's trying his best not to sneer. You haven't a clue as to why you feel so immediately attracted to him. "Harry Number Seven," you say, "give me three good reasons why I should pick you and then give me three better reasons why I shouldn't."

Harry Number Seven cracks a knowing grin. "You want

a reason? Fine. I'll give you just what you want. One: I enjoy cooking and cuddling. Two: I get along swell with my mother. Three: I have a magnetic personality, at least that's what it said in my last fortune cookie."

You notice he has nice teeth. Reason number four. "Answer the rest of my question, please."

"Oh," says Number Seven, looking dour. "Do I have to?"

The MC shrugs. "Sorry. Rules."

"Okay," says Number Seven. "It's kind of personal, but okay. Okay. One: I've been traded in hundreds of times. Two: You might say I've, er, uhm... had quite an effect on twelve of my last fifteen dates, at least that's what they tell me, the ones who can still talk, I mean."

There's a disapproving outburst from group the behind you and a couple of shoppers hurriedly leave the room.

Your heart races. "Reason number three?" you prompt.

Harry flashes a boyish grin meant to be endearing. It works. "Three," he says, "I don't have any regrets about anything I've done. Four: I'll do it again. To you, unless you stop me."

The lights go out and the MC blathers on about technical difficulties while the counselor refills your drinks. "How'd he get through screening?" someone asks, and a someone answers, "How did any of us?" In a few minutes, when the lights go back on, Harry Number Seven is gone. Gone, but not forgotten. Someone, you forget whom, once said, "Love Ain't Nothing But Hate Misspelled." It's taken a lifetime, but finally you see the logic in that statement.

There's no question about whom you will pick. Number Seven is a psychopath, but he could be your psychopath. You are convinced that he can make you feel alive, at least for a while. The two of you deserve each other, that much is obvious.

You mark down NUMBER SEVEN as your first, second, and third choice. He's got exactly what you want; he told you so himself, and even you know better than to keep looking for a poodle when there's a pit bull scratching at the door. Maybe it's finally time to let the dog come in.

You're turning over a new leaf. After all, Today is Your Lucky Day. For too many years you have been living on the edge, trying to straddle that line separating loser from victim. But no more. Because this Harry is the one you have been waiting for, the Harry with exactly what it takes to push you over.

STORYTIME

First appeared in *The MacGuffin*,
Spring, 2001

This story begins with a beautiful and happy woman whose husband is madly in love with her. The husband is a professional of some type, a doctor or scientist, or perhaps something to do with business. The woman is a stay-at-home mom, fulfilled and devoted to her family. There are two intelligent, well-behaved children: a teenage boy and his younger sister, each with twenty-twenty vision. The children's orthodontist has stated that no correction is necessary.

Not one neighbor has ever heard raised voices coming from the house. Not one has heard the woman cry, or heard the sister scream when she is shoved against the wall. Because no one has heard these things, we can assume they never happened.

Each night, the husband calls from work to say, "I am getting ready to leave. Is there anything I can bring home to make things easier for you?"

The woman—who has not only prepared dinner, but already set the table—answers, "Nothing." She knows the husband will surprise her anyway, with flowers or sparkling wine. He is a considerate man, a quality she greatly admires.

The woman attends to her children, who sit quietly in the spacious family room finishing homework.

"Hi, Mom," says the son. Without waiting for a reminder, the son excuses himself to take his shower. He saves hot water for his sister, who prefers a bath. Cheeks scrubbed clean, towels put away in the dirty laundry, the children ready their clothes for the next day. They ask the woman if she needs any help with dinner. When she says no they thank her for all her hard work on their behalf. "Smells delicious," says the son. He leads his sister to the door where they wait to greet their father.

I hope your husband calls before coming home from work. If not, I hope your husband bothers to come home from work, that is, if you have a husband. If you do not have a husband, then I hope you have a lover who treats you kindly. I am afraid to ask about your children.

Dinner is a sumptuous feast and the woman is complimented by all.

"To my wife," says the husband, proposing a toast.

The children smile and lift their milk glasses; when the daughter spills, the woman does not get angry, does not think of hitting her. The children empty their glasses and the son pours himself more milk. His father is happy that the son has seconds, for he is a growing boy, and must practice good nutrition. There is plenty of milk in the refrigerator, more than enough for breakfast. In fact, there is so much milk that no one resents it when the son pours yet another cup.

"Storytime," says the son. Though his sister is twelve, she still enjoys hearing him read. The son always reads happy stories that do not interfere with sleep. Tonight he reads the one about the happiest family in the world. It is not a true story, yet she likes to hear it again and again, maybe because it never changes.

The children say their prayers and turn out the lights.

The couple moves into the living room where a fire of black oak and Douglas fir crackles in the fireplace. The husband holds his wife dear and strokes her scented hair. He kisses her softly, and murmurs that he loves her.

I hope you have a husband who kisses you and loves your children, even when he is not really their father. I hope your children are healthy and you have enough to eat. I hope your story is a happy one. If your story is not a happy one, please don't be offended if I do not ask to hear it.

In another part of town lives a family more unfortunate than the first. A poor woman, who could have been the happy wife in another story heads this family, if things had turned out differently. As it is, she is not so pretty, and does not have any husband. She has a lover, but he is not so wonderful.

The poor woman has two children: a good son and a severely retarded daughter. The daughter cannot walk without help, cannot speak, and does not seem to hear anything that is said. Her eyes are half-closed; the medication she takes to control her seizures adds to her natural state of drowsiness. The other kids in the neighborhood make sport when the poor woman pushes the wheelchair around the block.

Not today, though. Today, the good son offers to take the poor woman's daughter for a walk. He will guide her wheelchair slowly while telling her the names of flowers and trees. He promises not to abuse or humiliate the girl, which the poor woman wants desperately to believe.

The poor woman pins a red bow to her daughter's hair. She changes her daughter's bib and gives the good son money to buy ice cream, just in case a truck with cheerful music drives by. "Thank you," she says to the good son. "You don't know how much I appreciate your help."

Usually, the poor woman spends her day caring for and feeding the girl, who does not know when to open her mouth. Today, the good son will take on that responsibility and the poor woman can relax. Perhaps the poor woman will use her time to read a book, or better yet, to write one. How often people have said, "You should write a book," and she has laughed at the idea. She decides on a long hot bath first. Seldom can she waste the afternoon as she does now. The heat from her bath gone, she lets the water drain, then dresses in clean clothes that have never become stained by dirty fingers gripping the fabric. She touches lipstick to her mouth and runs a brush through her hair so she will look presentable, should her lover arrive unannounced.

She sits at the kitchen table to write, but can think of only fantasy and lies. These lies, she supposes, are what others call fiction. There is no point in writing the truth: that she both loathes and loves her daughter. The poor woman refuses to admit what she does not want anyone to learn. No one wants to hear about it, anyway.

I need to revise the story. I did not wish to imply that the poor woman hates her daughter. This is too sad to think about, and I should not have given that impression. I wanted to make this a pleasant story, with touches of light humor throughout.

I just remembered that that first time the good son takes the poor woman's daughter out for a walk around the block, it is a sunny day.

There is one part of the story that the poor woman is too ashamed to admit; it's important enough that I will tell it.

Something secret happens each time the daughter is left alone with the good son. It happens again, and again, until one day, a doctor discovers the secret. A social worker calls to confront the poor woman. "There is a problem," the social worker says. "We need to set up a meeting."

When she learns that her daughter is pregnant, the poor woman panics. She testifies that she had no idea of what happened on those many afternoons when she left her daughter's care to someone else. It is doubtful her daughter knows the truth about the whole situation, for her awareness is limited. Though the poor woman feels shame for neglecting her daughter, she wonders if what happened really makes any difference.

"You *must* know something about it all," says the social

worker. She threatens to remove the poor woman's daughter unless the situation changes at once. "I would remove her now," the social worker says, "except that there isn't anywhere else to put her that's much better."

In the end, the poor woman has no choice but to accuse the good son. She accuses the good son, knowing that the guilty seldom pay for what they do.

This is not the way this story was supposed to happen.

It was wrong to accuse the good son when it was just as much the poor woman's fault. The poor woman knew all along what was happening, but chose to ignore it. No one else—only the good son—had ever offered to help care for her daughter. If that help came with a price, then who was better able to pay but the child who had sabotaged every chance the poor woman had to live a good life?

The poor woman hasn't been entirely honest about her story, so let me clear things up and say that it was not the son who did those things in secret, it was the poor woman's lover.

The way the story reads now, the lover was the one who caused the trouble. The lover stayed home with the retarded daughter to let the poor woman leave the house. This man volunteered to care for the girl: feed her, change her linens, bathe her, love her, impregnate her. The poor woman suspected this all along, but she was so desperately alone, so needy for a lover, any lover, that she let things be.

In the next scene, the good son argues with the poor woman and her lover. They fight and things are said, mean and hurtful things that make everyone feel awful. Before the poor woman can straighten these things out, the lover leaves.

The poor woman blames the good son for everything. He drops out of school and runs away. He abandons his mother, not caring if he will be written out of her story.

*

For many months, the poor woman looks outside her window and prays for her lover to come back and keep her company. She sometimes utters prayers for her son, but with less fervor.

If he does come back, she knows her lover will again want to take care of her daughter.

May God forgive her, if her lover returns, she *will* let him care for her daughter. It scares the poor woman to know she is so weak. What the good son did not understand, what the social worker will never understand, what no one can ever understand, is how lonely it has been for the poor woman. No other men have offered to keep her company since that terrible day twelve years ago, when her daughter was born.

This is not the story I started out to tell, and I would like to begin again. I would like to change the ending, though to change the ending, I might have to change the beginning and I am not sure how to do that. It is difficult to change the beginning when the end has already been written. I wonder if some stories are just too sad to tell and it's better to forget them.

There's one more thing else I should mention—about the baby. The baby dies before it can be born to the poor woman's daughter. Everyone is glad the baby dies. Even the social worker says this is for the best. The baby would have been severely deformed due to the medications that prevent the daughter from having seizures. There might have been an operation, possibly complications and pain. Besides, there isn't anyone in this story fit to care for a baby.

Some day I want to tell a story about brave and noble people who rise above their circumstances to overcome adversity. These things often happen in stories, even if they are fictions in real life.

In real life, the poor woman knows what is happening to her daughter, but does nothing to stop it. She loses control of her life as easily as a writer loses control of her story. We lie to protect our stories, telling only the good things, the things we know from experience others will want to hear. Because no one wants to learn about a poor woman letting terrible things happen to her helpless daughter. This does not show good character or strong conviction—qualities that, though greatly admired, are rare.

I don't mean to blame the poor woman for her faults. I only wish to understand her, because if I understood her, perhaps I would better understand myself. You see, the inspiration for this story came from a similar circumstance, one where I suspected, yet said nothing.

It wasn't really my story, which is why I didn't write about it. I was barely a witness and not in any way responsible. It happened my first day on the job as an aide in a nursing home. The girl was brain-damaged and incontinent; I had twelve other patients, all just as needy, and not enough time to care for them. The grandfather really seemed to love her, and wasn't loving attention better than neglect? I suppose I should say that I quit after two days over this, but in truth, I left because I didn't enjoy the work. I don't know if saying something then would have mattered; I don't know if it matters now. It's easier to forget and move on, and like I said, in the nursing home, just like in the story, no one knew for sure until much later.

The poor woman revises her story to make it say what she wants known. She finds this preferable to the truth. For the poor woman, truth is as terrible as lies. Sad things would continue to happen, even if the poor woman told the truth.

I might revise my story to give it a happy ending, telling only what I want to remember and leaving out the sad parts. That is how the poor woman copes so she can get on with her life. I feel this way as well. I don't want to read about the Holocaust and the murder of a million children, see a tearful man pushing his infirm grandmother in a wheelbarrow as they flee Bosnia, or hear about school shootings and the death of innocence. It's the same old story; tell me another one.

A poor woman has no son. She lives with a daughter who does not know her. Because her daughter does not know her, it is as if the poor woman lives alone. When the poor woman cries, no one hears it. As no one hears her cry, we can assume it never happens.

THAT JELLYFISH MAN
KEEPS A-ROLLIN

First appeared in *The Third Alternative*,
#29, 2002

Yessirree, that Jellyfish Man is more, much more, than a dirty old man, why he's one medical marvel of bio-engineering. There he goes now, a-rollin down that rotting roadway on his aluminum dolly, paddling with those stunted flippertip-hands, humping each and every pothole to his artificial heart's content. It's better than feeling up a girl, says he, the way his implants release those chemicals he calls endorfins from his whorefins.

Not too many like him these days. Most folks get their bones replaced with fancy schmancy alloys that let them stand proud, stand tall. Not so the Jellyfish Man, who thinks living low to the ground is just fine. He's pleased the ratty Uprights look down on him, disgusted with his tubes that suck up just what he needs from the ground. They don't like it, that's their problem, not his. No regrets, he likes to brag. No regrets at all.

He rolls over pavement, his innards protected from the elements by a thick and shiny coating that the doctors say was modeled after sharkskin. He fast-humps the rain-slick street like she was some Tijuana whore and not just oily asphalt laid by city workers back in those days when the city had workers. But lately he hasn't felt too good and that's why he scheduled an adjustment with the doctor. He rolls up to the stop where a black tank waits to take him to the VA hospital. A uniformed chauffeur will drive him and another old guy, an Upright named Joe. That tank is government shiny and outfitted with the latest and greatest available.

They move along. The Jellyfish Man can't even feel the ratty bumps along the road. To *get off*, he must hump a seatbelt buckle that's fallen to the floor-mat.

What a waste of a drive through this fine city, says he.

Upright Joe, sitting behind him, leans forward to ask, You call this fine? The country's gone to hell and it's all our fault for getting so old, for costing so much. Sometimes I wonder if we're doing right by living. Let me ask you somethin, says he. Ain't you ever bored down there? Don't you miss lookin out the window? Kissin your old lady?

Maybe I'll miss her in a week from Tuesday, says the Jellyfish Man.

Next week is the Thanksgiving, when he'll go to his daughter's—Ms. Upright's—place. Not for dinner mind you, just to talk. That ingrate girl don't think of having him over to eat. If his son was still alive, he'd make damn sure his Pop got a home-cooked supper now and again. Not that daughter, though, who still blames him for the accident that took her brother. Wasn't even his fault about the boy; it was the hospital's. After all, they managed to save the Jellyfish Man now, didn't they? So whose fault was it that the boy died? Not his, and that's for sure. Should have sued and made them pay when he had the chance. A man ain't supposed to outlive his child, why it was just plain wrong.

He and Upright Joe get to be roommates, and in a couple of hours time, maybe even pals. And why not? They share something in common—why they're veterans! They fought hard for their country and now their country fights hard for them. Mealtimes, Upright Joe perches on the edge of the bed to eat his food from a tray while the Jellyfish Man sucks dust balls and silverfish from the floor. The both of them have talked their doctors into writing prescriptions for government surplus muscatel. The Jellyfish Man slurps his up so fast he has to ask Upright Joe to pour a wee bit more from his bottle.

Just a little, says Upright Joe sounding resentful. They start a-talking and Upright Joe admits he's worried because he's been losing weight no matter how much food he eats.

Pity for him, thinks the Jellyfish Man, but nothing I can do about it anyway. Despite the drinking he has a hard time getting to sleep. He wonders if Upright Joe is awake right now, worrying about his surgery. These things usually don't get to him the way it does right now, and he doesn't understand the feeling. Worst that could happen: he could die, and so what? He don't care, and no one else does, neither. Nah, it must be something else, maybe just indigestion. Seems to take forever before morning and time to go under the knife.

See you on the outside, Upright Joe calls from his stretcher. He'll be done quicker than the Jellyfish Man, who is a touch more complicated case.

The nurse pushes the Jellyfish Man back to the operating room where a doctor asks, You want any anesthetic this time?

No, says the Jellyfish Man. He likes to feel each cut; gives him a bigger rush than pussy-humping on cocaine. The doctor aims his scalpel, asks the nurse to hold the retractors.

Wider, says the Jellyfish Man. He moans and groans as his arteries get routed out by some kazillion-dollar device that's no more than an overpriced ramrod, medical-grade.

Yeah, baby, says the Jellyfish Man. Yeah, Baby. After they sew him back up, he hears the nurse run to the sink and spill her guts. Pity the poor Uprights and their delicate stomachs; ain't his job to make things any easier for them.

By the time he gets back to the room, Upright Joe is gone. He wants to ask the nurses about Upright Joe, but not a one of them will talk to him. Odd, being surrounded by all these bodies and still feeling so alone.

After several days and several bottles, the nurses tell him it's check-out time. We're closing early for the Holiday, says they. Everybody's got to go home to eat their turkey.

Who needs turkey when the government will buy your muscatel? says the Jellyfish Man.

The nurses give him a goodbye drink and wish him lots of luck on the outside. The tank is waiting in front of the building; the driver helps him up. The Jellyfish Man can't wait to hear the latest gossip. So, whatever happened to the other guy? says he.

Old Joe? the driver says. Killed hisself day before yesterday. Some men can't be satisfied, no matter what.

Suicide, the old man's friend, says the Jellyfish Man. Despite himself, he misses Upright Joe.

Thought the old man's friend was what they called pneumonia, says the driver, who is still on his first life and don't know better.

Not any more, says the Jellyfish Man. Not any more. You want out of here you got to be a little more creative.

He and the driver have what the Jellyfish Man thinks is a good laugh over that one, but later, when the driver helps him down, he dumps the Jellyfish Man on the street, twisting a dolly wheel out of alignment before the alarm goes off.

What's happening here? asks a videocopper. Everything all right?

It was an accident, the driver says. I'm sorry, he says, but you can tell he isn't really.

Pity for them all. Uprights gotta work till they're a kazillion on account of old slobs costing so much money, thinks that Jellyfish Man. Well, isn't that a shame? Should have thought of that before.

He starts toward his place under the bridge, but dammit, if it isn't Thanksgiving Day, and already time to go uptown. His daughter has told him to come before two, as she's somewhere to go that evening. She tried real hard to make him come another day, but he insisted. He'll be damned to spend Thanksgiving all alone.

A videocopper slows an Upright transport to let the Jellyfish Man cross the street. When the Jellyfish Man jumps the curb his belly does a little flip-flop, so he slows down to let the nausea pass. He ought to be relaxed from all the muscatel, but the Jellyfish Man feels squeezed, like he's eaten something he can't quite digest. Probably just nervous. After all, the Jellyfish Man hasn't seen his daughter in some time. Maybe long enough the old girl even misses him.

Forward, rolling forward. The Jellyfish Man pulls close behind an Upright, who breaks into a jog. The guy must be going home to dinner; a chunk of bloody something falls to the ground.

Thanksgiving dinner. Yum, yum. Sure smells fine.

Before the Upright can turn back, the Jellyfish Man is all over the scrap of meat, flippers brushing against fur, blood, and gobs of creamy white fat.

Pity for the starving Upright, but finders keepers.

Besides, he figures, why should I find my own food when I can get an Upright to do it for me?

With that, the Jellyfish Man sucks everything up through his feeding tubes. The Upright screams STOP and the Jellyfish Man feels the cold from his shadow even before he feels the kick. A videocopper in an armored box shouts, Move along and leave that old man alone in his misery, so nothing else happens.

I'm sure you'll find some turkey, the Jellyfish Man tells the Upright. If not tonight then maybe in a week from Tuesday.

His innards ache, but pain never slows him down. Then he feels something heavy hit him on the back: the ratty Upright has gone and thrown a brick. A pressure valve bursts, shooting high-tech snot all over the cracked cement. Add that to the list of things to be repaired during the next adjustment. But first things first and now it's off to see that daughter, see if she's changed her tune about her old man.

The videocopper's lights are shining every which way. The Jellyfish Man spies a leathery maple leaf and scoots that way.

Pretty thing—how it sweats in the rain, the edges all curled up— reminds him of lace undies. Feels good under his wheels, fragile yet crunchy. Been a cold winter, though the Jellyfish Man never bothers about the weather. Ratty Uprights are the only ones who care about staying warm.

Trash is piled up on the sidewalk to his right and even though he's running late, the glint of something sharp pokes out through the rubble and beckons like a painted woman. Slow down, he tells himself. Take time smelling them ratty roses. He jumps the curb and practically comes right there from the jolt. He humps that pile of trash, back and forth, back and forth, trying his best to hit the sharpies head-on.

Hey baby, says he. Nice to meet you.

His belly flops over the edge of the dolly he leased from the VA. There's only the one condition (like there always is with the VA)—that the lease be renewed every ninety-nine years, give or take. The Jellyfish Man knows the government's gotta have rules and regulations or it wouldn't be the government. As it was, he had quite a time convincing the VA to replace the standard-issue alloy wheels on his dolly with antique wooden casters. The old style let him feel the shock of the roadways much better than those high-falootin technological dickfors. Funny how old things cost so much more than something new, but that's the government for you, chargin you aplenty for peanuts and givin away the caviar for free.

Onward he travels, dipping into potholes, rising over bumps that trigger off pain and pleasure sensors on the order of once every fifteen seconds. The feeling is one of being prodded by electrical currents, but hey, at his age, the Jellyfish Man figures you take whatever you can without complaining. He swerves to hump some refuse that's started to go bad. He's grown to love the taste of scrap iron and swill, the sour smell of wet paper.

It don't get no better than this.

He heads into an alley belly-high in litter and broken bottles, and bumps along past his old house. The house has been turned into a Factory Training Center for Upright kids, what they used to call a school back in his day.

Glad they found a use for it. Never did like that house anyway. Wife, Delores, picked it out. Stupid woman. Pity for her. Died the day before they come out with immortality. Bet she woulda had her bones redone with that trendy liquid metal crap instead of silicone, just so's she could tower over him for eternity. If you asked him, the Jellyfish Man would tell you he really don't miss her much.

Hell, she'd stopped givin it to him since the menopause. Yessirree, when he thinks about it he's glad that woman's too dead to give him more of the same Homo Erectus shit instead of what he really wants. Now there's just the daughter, who is bossier than her mother ever knew how. He tells himself he's only going so as not to hurt her feelings, it being a holiday, and all. He sure don't love that brat, her and her ratty Upright sensibilities. Still, now and then he's tempted to give her another chance. She is his only family, after all.

Pity his son had to go an die before the miracle of regeneration. Who could forgive doctors who didn't do a damn thing to save the boy's life? The Jellyfish Man sometimes wonders if things might have been a little different had his son survived that car crash. The wife blamed him, said it was his fault for drinking, said he was the one who deserved to die. Everybody blamed him for all their troubles. Bet ya if that old dead biddy could see him now, she'd be singing a different tune!

Uprights. Hump em all. They could keep their never-ending jobs, decrepit commuter transports, sardine can apartments. The Jellyfish Man likes things this way, likes living by himself under a bridge. Kind of back to the earth, primal even. He don't owe the world a thing.

He turns down the street that leads to his daughter's place and rolls on toward the building. He intimidates an Upright into holding the front door while he humps the threshold three or four times in a row.

135

That humping relieves some of the pressure that's been bugging him all morning, but then something new starts to crawl inside him. It's that daughter of his. What a pain she's turned out to be. Women. Who needs 'em, anyway?

The Upright calls for the elevator and the Jellyfish Man rolls a little too close to the guy's feet than is polite. This one's got real shoes, must be an executive. The Jellyfish Man reaches over to casually hump the leather with his flipper, greatly appreciating the chewy taste. His innards still gurgle from that bit of fatty meat and he's not surprised when the Upright decides against riding up with him and rushes off to take the stairs instead.

Lucky man. If he could, the Jellyfish Man would be humping along those steps himself going up and down, up and down. Up and down. Yessirree, that would be something.

Finally, the elevator door slides open and the Jellyfish Man gets on. The buttons are low enough and he presses every one to get as many bumps as possible. He rides on up to Maggie's floor and rolls toward number 1512. The carpet smells like sanitized dirt, dogs, and talcum, but the texture is nice—soft but kind of scratchy.

Ahead of him the door opens and he spies Maggie's slender legs peeking out from her skirt. That gal is still single, though she's nearly sixty. She's had most of her bones and joints redone so she can keep doing her ballet. Says she'd work even if she didn't have to, but he don't believe that. Why would anybody work, if they had the choice?

How you doin, Pop?

He rolls into her place without an answer, sniffing out what's new and what's changed.

She don't say nothing for a long time so he figures it's hard for her to gather up her nerve and ask what she surely wants to ask: for her Pop to stay for dinner. Maybe what she needs is a shot of something to break the ice.

Got a drink for me? says he and he can feel a shudder in the floor as her toes pump the carpet through her shoes.

I don't think that's such a good idea, says she.

Come on, girlie. Why you gonna deny your old man his due? he asks.

He starts to roll around, bumping into the walls and leaving wet streaks against the paint. He sniffs everywhere to find her liquor until at last she gives in.

Okay, says she. Okay. What would you like?

Whiskey, says he. Put it in a glass bowl, not one of them aluminum pie tins. Leaves an aftertaste. Why even bother if it don't taste right? One of my few pleasures, says he, chortling, because he can't admit the other, her being his kid and all.

Yes, Pop, says she.

She goes to a cabinet and fiddles with the latch for what seems like forever before she gets around to pouring him something. She covers a square of carpet with blue plastic and slides the glass dish over that.

He rolls right over and sticks his flippers all the way inside that dish, desperate to suck up every last drop.

That sure is good, says he. Got any more?

A little, says she, but he can tell she's none too happy.

She don't like him drinking, but there's more to it than that. There's something she wants to tell him but dammit she don't say a word. Pretty soon, his stomach seizes up and he rolls around to get things working again.

Pour me another drink, says he, making his voice as loud as he can.

No more, says she, almost begging. That stuff is gonna kill you.

Unlikely, says he, but don't you wish? Maybe just a little? Nights especially, he wouldn't mind dying all that much himself.

She starts up crying and says, Please don't say that, Pop.

Girlie, says he, you know I'm only a-kiddin.

It's not very funny, says she, but she fills up the dish anyway.

She clears her throat like she's finally ready to speak. Pop, says she. She blows her nose and says, You got anywhere to go for

Thanksgiving Turkey?

I knew it, says he, and for the first time all day his gut stops aching. That girl still loves him after all! First dinner and after that she's gonna ask him to live with her! He'd hate to admit to anyone how much he likes that idea, but really, it makes the most sense of anything. He does, at times, get lonely.

He rolls around in a circle that stops at her feet. He's feeling snug and warm inside, and not just from the whiskey. He looks around and chooses the corner by the window that will soon be his. I don't got nowhere to go, says he. Hint hint.

You ever think about asking somebody to take care of you? says she.

You got yourself a pretty nice place, he answers. Guess I might not mind moving in, so long as you don't try to feed me any vegetables.

Then that Upright daughter of his gasps and stamps her foot.

No! says she and he sees a look of horror in her eyes. What do you mean stay with me? says she. What in the world are you talking about? Color drains from her face and stains the sleeve around her armpits like she's bleeding, except its sweat.

His gut squeezes shut again and he tries to talk, but can't. At last he manages to whisper, You are asking me to come stay, ain't you?

No! She screams, and backs away. That's not what I meant. I was talkin about a home, Pop! Someplace nice where they'd take care of you, keep you clean and out of trouble. Someplace where they'd feed you a decent Thanksgiving dinner.

The Jellyfish Man feels wobbly, like he's about to lose every last drop of hooch right there on her carpet.

No thank you, says he. Put me in a home, will ya? No! And I mean no!

Way he's heard it, folks have up and died in them kind of homes. He tells her he don't intend to die before his time, which could be never.

Pop! She's practically weeping. You can't be happy the way you are.

Her pity hurts him more than if she'd stabbed him in the heart. So why don't this feel good, like other kinds of pain?

He tries to act like it was all a mistake. Be a darlin now, says he in his calmest voice, and pour your old man another drop of rye.

Takes some time for her to settle down, but of course, she does it. He is her flesh and blood, when everything's been boiled down to the basics.

Their visit ends and Maggie walks the Jellyfish Man to the door and says Goodbye in a slow voice, like she's sad to see him go. Come visit me again, says she. I'll save you some scraps.

Maybe in a week from Tuesday, says he with a bitter laugh.

He tells himself he feels nothing at all for her. Not love, not duty, not nothin. Who needs family? Not him! He's happy as a clam all by himself. He's always finding the treasures that the Uprights drop, and like he's said a kazillion times, there's sex anytime he wants it.

I'm a man-o-war. King-o-the-sea. This life tops the first life by a mile.

Hooch has got him so relaxed he don't think twice about dumping right in front of Maggie's place. He cleaned up plenty after her, when she was a baby, after all. Her turn, now. Always will be. Last laugh's on her for letting an old fart like me live forever in the first place.

The Jellyfish Man presses the down button and feels a smile begin in his belly. He's glad the elevator goes so creaky slow because there's a wad of spearmint gum stuck to the floor that takes a little longer than usual to work free.

Man, that minty bite sure tastes fine.

Outside the building, the Jellyfish Man rolls across the sidewalk toward the curb. He zooms down the apron, which slopes into the oily street. His flippers brush a mound of gray pebbles and he wonders why it is so many shades of dark come out at night. This block is his new favorite, really rough, chock full of potholes. One of the worst in the city. Humping this street makes the trip almost worthwhile.

Uprights. They're the only ones who still complain. Only three of them on the tax rolls for every one of him. Serves 'em right, it does. They're only gettin what they deserve. Should've saved my boy when they had their chance, then maybe I'd be singin a different tune. But I ain't got no regrets, he thinks. Too late for that now.

The Jellyfish Man ignores the gurgling in his gut that turns to a throbbing pain and reaches clear from head to tail. If he can't find a way to hump it, he'll just bide his time and get the pain fixed at the VA.

A videocopper blows an electronic whistle and the transport traffic grinds to a halt long enough to let the Jellyfish Man cross the street. So what if that Upright daughter of his didn't ask him to stay for dinner? It ain't her duty to take care of him. He wouldn't have traded his freedom for her companionship, anyhow.

He remembers back forty years, when his son was hardly cold in the ground and the doctors tried to talk to him about immortality. No way was he gonna take the Man-O-Steel approach like everybody else. What kind of father did they think he was anyway, offering him perfection when his only boy was dead?

There's a broken glass bottle in the gutter. He rolls over to hump it, feeling grateful for the distraction. He humps the glass, humps it again and again. Humps it to death until he can taste himself bleeding, until he can feel the pain where the sharpies have broken through his shiny coating. When he's numb with pain he heads back toward his bridge.

Worthless Upright daughter. The Jellyfish Man turns down the alley that used to be his alley and scours the street for something good to eat. He never looks up and never looks back, why even if he wanted to, t'would be practically impossible, the way they've got him configured. He just keeps a-rollin forward, ever forward, over the bumpy streets of the city and into the dark wet night.

THE CHANGELING

First Appeared in *Lady Churchill's Rosebud Wristlet* #13

My boyfriend's nickname was Spot because of his condition—vitiligo—which bleached pigment from his dark skin, leaving erratic white patches that made no sense. He hated the nickname. I wanted to call him "Domino," but the people who cared hardly ever chose nicknames, so I used his real name, Steve.

I didn't know he had so many spots until I saw him without clothes, which wasn't until our fourth date. By then I was in love and imperfections didn't matter. I'd never been with a black guy; for all I knew, spots were normal. Steve had been with white women, but was polite enough not to compare, even when asked. Steve said his white spots complemented my freckles. We both believed our differences were no big deal.

Last Monday, I threw up on the futon and had to tell him: I was pregnant. Fourteen weeks, by calendar count. I wiped the sheets but one stain was stubborn, no matter how hard I scrubbed.

"Forget it," Steve said. "Want coffee?"

"Sure," I said. I threw that up, too.

"Anyway, you aren't supposed to drink coffee," Steve said. He rubbed my belly to help my stomach settle.

"I think you mean alcohol," I said. I wasn't ready to give up coffee.

Steve was wearing red shorts and a white terry robe belted at

141

the waist. His chest was chocolate-sauce smooth and he looked boxer strong and handsome. I pretended the white spots on his chest weren't there. "What do you want to do?" Steve asked.

I didn't know. "Do you love me enough to get married?" I asked.

"I don't know. Do you love me that much?"

The day before, I would have said yes. I said yes anyway.

"Then let's get married," he said. "For the baby."

"For the baby," I said.

We got dressed and went to work. Steve managed World CD and I clerked at U.S. Jeans.

When I called my mother on my break, she said, "Get an abortion."

"It's one thing to have sex with one, but I don't think I could ever love the child," Mom said. "Neither black nor white. Unfair to give a child problems to begin with."

I yelled, said she was prejudiced and hung up the phone. Steve's parents felt no different about me than Mom did about Steve. I'd make Steve tell them the news.

The rest of the day was customer hell; at closing, the register was short sixteen dollars. When I came home, Steve told me to sit and wouldn't let me help make dinner.

I worried I was making a mistake. Every baby deserved to be loved, especially mine. "Maybe we shouldn't get married," I said.

"You aren't thinking of abortion?" he said. "Because I think that's murder."

"No," I said, even though I wasn't sure I wanted a baby.

"Good," said Steve. "I mean, it's your body. But it *is* half my baby."

That night I dreamt of babies half black and half white, split midway down the centers like jester hats.

In the morning we had sex and it was good. After, Steve held me and tenderly rubbed my belly. I loved almost everything about him: the way he talked, his thoughtfulness, the CD art hanging on his walls, the way he looked in clothes, and the way he felt out of them. I loved his body and how his skin felt waxy like polished jade, except for those bleached spots. I loved how he took the lumpy side of the futon and gave me the better half.

"How about some green tea?" he said.

"In a bit," I answered.

My stomach felt calm so long as I didn't stand up. Too bad I had to work. Clearance sale today; at least busy days passed faster.

I started to cry without a reason.

Steve whispered, "It'll be okay, baby."

By baby he meant me and not the baby.

There was a white spot near his navel and I touched it. My fingers traced the perimeter and then sneaked inside to explore the white circle. It felt bumpy there. Not like normal skin. "Will they ever come out?" I asked. "The spots?"

"This is who I am," Steve said, sounding grouchy. "Get used to it."

"I will," I said. "I am. I'm sorry."

Steve said, "I forgive you. Hey, I got the name of a doctor. We're gonna need prenatal care."

"Oh, yeah," I said. The baby. I wanted my prenatal care from a kit, like my pregnancy test. I didn't want strangers looking into places I couldn't see myself.

I propped up on my side and stared at Steve and pictured him as a father and not a lover. There was something wrong with the picture. He looked the same. Whereas I would soon look fatter.

I let Steve shower first so I could lie still as long as possible. I stared at my belly to see if I was showing, but couldn't tell. I wouldn't have known I was pregnant if my boobs weren't sore and my periods hadn't stopped and I didn't feel like throwing up and if all three home pregnancy tests hadn't been positive. Maybe Steve's doctor would order a sophisticated test that instead proved I had tumors.

I showered and dressed in jeans and a white tee shirt. Steve brought me saltines and I ate them and sipped tea and managed to keep both down. I rode the bus to work, standing to give my seat to a woman with a tiny baby. The woman had caught me staring, so I felt I should say *something*. I said, "Isn't it cute!" even though it wasn't.

Customers lined up half an hour before we opened. My manager said, "Just keep smiling," when one pounded on the windows, pointed to her watch, and mouthed something nasty. The morning passed sunrise quick. The starchy sizing scent of new clothes made me sick and I threw up twice. On my lunch break, I made the doctor's appointment. The chatty receptionist said the doctor was white but from South Africa. I felt glad, then guilty for feeling glad, and hung up to look through the phone book for a doctor who was black. None of the ads had pictures, except of chiropractors, so I stayed with the first guy.

On the bus home, I gave up my seat to a retarded girl who might have been pregnant or just fat. Either way, people looked angry with her. Someone said, "People like that shouldn't have children."

That pissed me off. I said, "Don't be so judgmental!" Then I decided that the retarded girl was just fat, and I got mad at her, too.

Steve was away at practice; he played bass in an alternative band. I felt trapped in a mood where nothing held my attention and I kept flipping channels with the remote. I couldn't commit to a television show. Was I crazy to think I could commit to a husband and a baby? Eventually, the batteries died; I solved that by sitting close enough to the TV to change channels with my feet.

My mom called.

"Oh," I said. "It's you."

"Is something wrong?" she asked and I said no because really, when you thought about it, there wasn't. I was in love. I was pregnant. Didn't everyone want to get married and have a baby?

"I was a bit harsh," she said. "About the baby. I'm sure I'll come to accept it," she said.

"It's not about you!" I said.

"True," she said, without asking how I felt.

I left serial messages on Steve's cell phone, then waited for a callback. He didn't call, but showed up around one, saying he hadn't wanted to take a chance on waking me.

We snuggled in bed.

"I thought you wanted to talk," he said when it was obvious I was going to say zip.

"I do," I said, not knowing what to say. We fell asleep and I woke up before him and watched his profile bloom in the morning light.

If only Steve didn't have spots! My fingers walked along his skin until they found a small white circle on his thigh. I'd never noticed it before, because of his leg hair. I'd thought I already knew everything about him, so this new spot bugged me. I wasn't paying attention and didn't notice when I started to rub harder, with as much pressure as I'd used to scrub the sheets. My fingers dug into his skin like a number four eraser trying to snuff marks left by a number two pencil.

Steve said, "Ouch!" and I saw I'd drawn blood. "Baby," Steve said, "what the hell are you doing?"

"I don't know," I said. "I wasn't thinking."

"Well, think," he said with a laugh. "For my sake, think."

He stared at his leg and said, "Jesus, what did you do?"

I apologized for making him bleed. Except it was worse. Instead of the white patch disappearing into the black as I would have expected, I had erased the surrounding dark pigment and made the white part spread.

"I didn't mean to," I said. I tried to push away all thoughts that it might be easier if Steve was white.

"Oh, man," he said with a sigh. "Think you're the only one who worries we'll face problems?"

"Our differences don't matter."

"Is that right?" he said. "I don't believe you."

I didn't believe me either, which scared me.

145

Steve said, "We should see a counselor."

"It's too late for talk."

"I suppose you're right," Steve said.

Because Steve disliked rubbers, I was having a baby. This wasn't fair! I stared at the insensitive, selfish man I was about to marry. Maybe he wouldn't be such a good father after all. I climbed atop him and scrubbed the white patch on his chest.

"Please stop," he said, but I kept at it until I made the white spot stretch.

"I can't handle this!" he said. "Why should I change and not you?"

"Go ahead?" I said, letting go.

Steve held my arm and picked at a freckle on my arm. Massaging the brown spots with his thumbs made the color break open and seep into the white. He darkened a full moon across my shoulder before stopping. "There," he said. "How's that feel?"

It felt wrong.

I touched Steve's new white patches. They felt bay leaf dry. "Shit!" I said. "I'm so sorry!" I really was.

"This is stupid," he said.

"No duh," I said.

I laughed and so did he. Our first fight; no wonder we weren't any good at it.

I rubbed big circles over my tummy, wondering if that could make the baby change colors. Steve patted my tummy so gently that I knew he didn't mean anything by it. "Even if you turned me white or I turned you black, this baby's made," Steve said.

"I'm not ready," I said.

"Me neither," said Steve.

"Oh well," I said.

"Exactly," said Steve.

I remembered why I loved him. I felt something weird from inside that began as a tickle and grew stronger, like a skater tracing a figure eight into the ice. "The baby!" I said. It was kicking with its tiny feet. Was it was trying to change me, the way babies did, from the inside, in ways you couldn't see?

"Let's call it, Domino," I said. "You know—baby topples the stack."

"Good one," said Steve. "The question is, do we stand by and watch or do we try to stop the fall?"

"No question," I said, hugging him tight.

"You're right," he said.

I felt happy. We both stared at my belly, curious, maybe a little scared, and waited, helpless to do anything but watch for the baby to make its next move.

THE WERESLUT OF AVENUE A

First appeared in *Bending The Landscape 3*,
Overlook Press, May, 2001

It was that time of the month again when Agatha was about to go animal and there wasn't a damn thing Helen could do, except wait for it to be over.

Such was the nature of their relationship.

Helen knew Agatha was older, but not how much. She knew Agatha had loved others, but not how many. Helen was twenty-one and Agatha was the only woman she had loved, truly loved.

Agatha often said that love was not enough.

At times, like now for instance, Helen almost believed her.

Agatha stood at the window, peering out at the night. Her apartment was a sparsely decorated fifth floor walkup.

It had been over an hour since she had arrived home from work, yet Helen was still breathless. She could not take her eyes from Agatha, always so lovely. She was wearing a pink satin nightgown, seemingly nothing underneath. Helen was dressed in jeans and a loose flannel shirt. Helen thought about ripping off Agatha's clothes, sucking on her perfect nipples. Even when Agatha was on her moon, Helen wanted sex.

Agatha wanted sex, too. Just not with Helen.

"I'm sorry it has to be this way," Agatha said. She closed the blinds, turned toward Helen. "It's time," she said. Her hair was long and blonde, tied back to frame a shiny face shaped full and pale like the moon. She smiled, her reassuring everything-will-be-okay smile.

Things would not be okay, not for Helen. There were too many differences between them. That shouldn't have mattered, but did.

"Tie me up," Agatha said.

The wire crate beside the bed held the hard restraints Agatha needed for tonight. Helen's hands shook. She was a big woman, but sometimes, Agatha made her feel small.

"It's time," Agatha said again, irritation in her voice.

She hesitated. "Why does it have to happen?" Helen asked.

Agatha shrugged, walked closer. "I don't know," she said. She touched Helen's cheek with the back of her hand. "Some things just are."

"Let me kiss you," Helen said.

Agatha smiled, brought her face close.

Helen parted the dry lips with her tongue, licked the elegant teeth hidden within. Her tongue swam lazily in the warm sea of her lover's mouth. She grabbed Agatha's ass and rubbed against her.

Agatha humored her for a few seconds before pulling away. "That's enough," she said.

It was not easy to let go. "Okay," Helen said. She closed her eyes, took one deep breath followed by another. She stared at Agatha, inflamed, infatuated.

"It's time," Agatha said. "Past time."

"Okay," Helen said. "Lie down."

It was unclear at first whether Agatha had heard. Then, without meeting Helen's glance, she obeyed.

Helen removed a set of thick straps from the crate. The leather was discolored by sweat, the grain worn smooth in places and the bronze buckles blackened by time. She remembered early on—when they were first together—Agatha's change imminent, Helen's excitement upon seeing the leather. It had all seemed like a game. with Agatha the master and Helen the willing student.

Agatha lay on her back now, hips forming peaks beneath the fabric of her gown. The satin clung to her, an illusory skin, supple and soft, yet colder to the touch than river water.

Helen reached to stroke her rounded belly.

Agatha pushed her away, her grip surprisingly strong. "No!" she cried. "Not now." She spread her legs to let Helen slip a strap around each foot. Her calves were muscular, tanned.

Helen counted by twos, then by sevens to take her mind from Agatha. When that didn't work, she squeezed shut her eyes until Agatha appeared foggy, a mirage. Still, she sensed her there, more intoxicating than ever. Agatha's breath smelled of wine, her skin of citrus.

Helen watched the pulse in Agatha's neck rise and fall with the delicate grace of butterfly wings. She thrust one hand between Agatha's thighs, leaned forward.

Agatha slugged her hard in the jaw. "Tie me up," she said.

The taste of blood was sobering. "Sorry," Helen said, sitting upright. She pulled the leather through the buckle, gave it a firm tug.

"Tight as you can," Agatha commanded

She gave it another pull. Then she shackled one foot to the bedpost, followed by the other, leaving Agatha's arms for last.

Agatha did not speak or move, even after Helen said, "I love you." She straddled Agatha's waist and tied her hands. "I want to kiss you," she said.

"Not now," Agatha said. "After. When it's over."

By then Helen might not want her. Defeated, she rubbed against her, roughly enough to snag the satin with her zipper.

"Chill," Agatha said. "This has nothing to do with you."

"I keep forgetting that," Helen said. She dismounted, brought her fingers to her lips, blew a kiss. The scent of leather lingered on her hands, as if she had wrestled with some beast but managed to grab only a small part of it for herself.

Agatha sighed. "Turn on the radio, Helen. Loud. Lock the doors. No matter how I scream or what I say, you mustn't let me loose."

"I know the drill," Helen said, and followed Agatha's instructions.

The radio was set to an oldies station, and the music went on and on about loving the one you were with.

"How convenient," Helen said. She turned up the sound and watched silently as Agatha glowered. She perched at the edge of the bed, staring, utterly unable to understand what was happening or even why she allowed herself to be used like this.

The change progressed rapidly from then on. Agatha perspired, her nails grew into claws. Her breasts became engorged, her lips red and puffy. She exuded a musky smell not meant for Helen. Agatha lifted her hips, moaned. "Helen, you've tied me too tight." She pulled at her restraints. "I need to get away," she said. "Just for a while. Let me go."

Helen wanted to fuck her more than ever.

"Let me loose!" Agatha screamed.

"No," Helen said. "This was your idea, remember?" Funny, how Agatha was in bondage, yet she was the slave. Things were never as they seemed. Never.

"Forget what I said. I've changed my mind," Agatha said. "Let me go." Her eyes shone; she panted with excitement. "I'm hungry for others," she said. "You can't keep me here for yourself."

"No," Helen said. "It's just the moon talking."

Agatha bared her teeth. "It's not the moon. It's you. You're not enough to satisfy me."

"Don't say that," Helen said. "You'll feel better in a few days." She pulled the straps tighter, determined not to let her get away. Imagining Agatha in the arms of another, she changed, from hurt, to despair, to anger. She fondled a nipple the way she might caress a trigger.

Agatha spat in her face. "I'll get away," she said. "You don't own me."

"No," Helen said, "that much is obvious."

Helen wanted to cause pain. Except that Agatha was the cruel one.

"I'm bleeding," Agatha said, glancing downward. "Look how they cut into me!" She sounded pitiful.

Her wrists were red and swollen. "All right," Helen said, and loosened her bonds. Agatha reached up to grasp her hands, leaving Helen feeling giddy. One touch, and Helen was ready to forgive everything.

"Say that you love me," Helen said, a doggish whimper. She buried her nose in Agatha's bosom to fill her lungs with her sweet scent.

"No!" Agatha said. "I don't love you."

It was a lie; Helen did not believe it. Her face felt heavy, stiff as a leather mask. She stood up to pace the length of the room.

"You do love me," Helen said. "You've just forgotten." She walked to the door, unwilling to witness the transformation any longer. "I'll be back," she said.

Agatha howled. "Let me go! You've no right to keep me here! I don't belong to you. You can't keep me! You can't!"

"I know," Helen said, and headed toward the kitchen for a drink. There, she twisted open a Samuel Adams, drained nearly half the bottle before pausing for a breath.

Agatha called after, "You've no right!"

Then Helen heard the tinkle of broken glass followed by a heavy thudding as Agatha clambered down the fire escape. Her lover was gone, which came as no surprise.

Desire had no hold on a creature like that. Helen leaned over the table, head cupped in hands. God! she thought. What am I to do?

She called in sick to work the next day, and the day after.

Her supervisor threatened her; some emergency at work, some problem with the equipment, but Helen didn't care. It seemed important that she be there when Agatha returned.

Sleep was a ridiculous goal. She stayed awake, almost until morning. In the middle of the fourth night, she heard Agatha climb in through the open window.

Relief washed through her.

Agatha slipped beneath the covers to lay beside her.

Helen feigned sleep, afraid to make the first move.

Suddenly, Agatha's hands were on her everywhere.

Helen pretended to awaken at their touch.

Agatha's gown was moist, with a wild scent clinging to her like smoke. Her hair was matted and damp. She mounted Helen, slid her hands over Helen's stomach, and rubbed her groin against Helen's.

"Honey," Agatha said, "I'm home."

In a moment, both were panting and rollicking in the bed. Tongues and fingers darted inside and outside one another. They wept, moaned, licked, and fucked long past that first delicious squeeze and release signaling orgasm.

When Agatha fell into sleep, her breathing changed to the low timbre of wind through a barely closed window.

Helen stayed awake. Already, she anticipated the pain of the next time.

Then it happened: one full moon, Agatha asked Helen to change, become a creature like her.

They were sitting together on the couch. She took Helen's hands in hers.

"The way I am is killing you," she said. "And I can't stand to watch you suffer because of who I am. The answer is to join me. Change, or I'll have to let you go."

"No!" Helen said. "You should be the one to change."

"I can't," she said. "I won't. So it has to be you. I want you to see others," she said. "Maybe then you won't be so jealous." Agatha took such joy in controlling her.

"I want no others," Helen said. "I only wish you felt the same."

Agatha shrugged. "I'm not like you," she said. "You knew that when you met me. I've been honest about what I was."

That was true. Helen looked away, embarrassed at the futility of her deepest wish—that Agatha be faithful.

She had to ask. "Why am I not enough for you?"

"You are enough," Agatha said, with a dismissive wave. "It's just that I want more."

She treated her like child.

"Why do you care," Helen asked, "if I'm like you or not?"

Agatha laughed. "I'm tired of your moping and dependence," she said. "You'd be happier seeing others."

"It's you who would be happier," Helen said. "Because then you'd feel free to do as you pleased without thinking of me. Well, maybe I want you to feel guilty."

"But I won't feel guilty," Agatha said. "I will never feel guilty. That's what kills you."

Agatha was right. It was killing her.

When Agatha smiled, her eyes glittered.

Helen wanted to get back at her.

"You've got to change," Agatha said. "It's for your own good, because I care about you. Otherwise, I really think that we should call it quits."

Helen did not doubt she would carry out her threat, abandon her for a stranger.

"All right," Helen said. "I'll change. But how?"

Agatha wrapped her legs around Helen's and squeezed. "It will hurt," she said, "but only for a while."

It already hurt.

She led Helen to the bed, but did not reach for the box with the leather restraints. Instead, Agatha pushed her down, lay atop her. As Helen nuzzled her lips against Agatha's cheek, Agatha lowered her mouth to Helen's neck and bit her, hard and deep.

Helen screamed, trembled, sweated, convulsed. Her body grew tense; when she looked at her arms, she saw the hair was growing into a black thicket. The colors in the room ran together like moistened chalk. She was lightheaded and soon lost track of time. She understood how it felt to be possessed.

Her change seemed to drive Agatha wild with passion. She fumbled with Helen's belt, tugged clumsily at her jeans.

She managed to unbutton the fly, but gave up pulling the

pants all the way off.

Helen could not command her hands to help get undressed.

Agatha brushed Helen's vulva with her nose. "You smell nice," she said; the buzz of lips tickled. "Very nice." She lapped at Helen's clitoris until her tongue had turned it to stone.

Helen awakened fully then and held Agatha's head steady. Agatha strained against her grip, but did not let go until Agatha had satisfied her.

Agatha licked her lips and fingers and turned languorously on her back. She wore the smile that usually melted Helen. She rubbed her neck, chided Helen for being so rough. "Now me," she said, raising her arms above her head. She spread her legs, lifted her hips.

Helen stood and fixed her clothes while Agatha writhed about on the bed. Agatha's earthy scent was exciting, repellant, made her hot, left her cold.

Helen wanted sex, just not with Agatha.

She walked to the window and gazed out at the bone china moon, a teacup in an iridescent saucer.

"I'm going out," Helen said. She imagined the taste of others on her fingers, women, soft, moist.

"No!" Agatha said. "You can't leave!"

Helen laughed, but did not glance back.

"What about me?" Agatha cried.

Helen realized seconds before Agatha that it was over between them.

The feeling passed over her like a shadow traveling across a canyon.

Helen could no longer remember what she had ever seen in Agatha. "You'll manage," she said.

GOING VAMPIRE

First appeared in *Realms of Fantasy,*
December, 1998

My name is Victor Di Lorenzo and I've been a Hollywood agent for too long now, a vampire for maybe half that. I first got, what we say in my biz, the call, way back when, from a Lucille Ball look-alike desperate for companionship. Once bitten I was smitten, which worked out okay. I was never much of a morning person.

Lucy and me had a rocky relationship that got worse after she went over. Going over—that's an expression vamps use when somebody loses it, when they give up on the life. The blood, the never-ending hunger, the secrecy takes its toll, and don't let anyone tell you different. Lucy went over, bailed out almost ten years ago, when she looked into the sun. I've been alone ever since.

So no one was more surprised than me to learn that things don't have to be that way, that I'm still capable of love. Last night, I'm working the night shift at LAX. I'm starving 'cause I ain't eaten too good for a week or so, walking through the concourse wishing there was blood takeout. My feet are pounding a drum roll on the blue pavement (as I think of the carpet). I'm checking all around for vamps or other agents on the troll when I see the girl deplane. Too young for me, not that age matters worth bean sprouts when you live forever. Taller by a hand, nice body, good hair, just the wrong color. Deep set brown eyes with painted-on lashes that remind me of Twiggy. The look of someone vulnerable yet fully capable of knocking down a sorry old fool like me.

I do maybe ninety percent of my recruiting at the airport, have a pretty good system for picking up clients. They gotta have the look or I can't do nothing with them. Attractive enough to thumb their noses at low-budget porn offers but not so beautiful or talented as to stand a real chance in the industry. Secure in their abilities, yet realistic. It helps if they got an IQ above seaweed. I don't like taking unfair advantage of anybody. After all, I got my scruples. Likely, because of my blood habit, I also got someone else's.

So, this girl hoists her carry-on bag to her chest—that suitcase-armor thing so many females do—stops walking and looks all around her like she don't believe she's finally here.

Some guy coming up behind her has his mug behind a Wall Street Journal and bumps into her. "Good place to stop, asshole," he growls, but she don't seem to notice or care.

I know exactly how she's feeling. She's left her hometown and everything she's ever known, been in airports or on planes all day. She's tired; her back aches and she's long past feeling excited about her future.

It's been a while, but I remember that final descent into LA, how the plane drops through the layer of smog engulfing the San Gabriel Mountains, how that smog looks like clouds on fire, how you're thinking: here I am—the hole where Heaven meets Hell.

Here's the funny thing: once you land, you stop noticing the smog. You look up and realize all you can see of those dark clouds are memories. Which should be a warning.

This girl looks appropriately scared, but brave. She's got that real look to her, something that's hard to fake. I'm positive I can get her into a sanitary napkin commercial or two, and if I'm lucky, maybe hand cream, enough to keep her hoping that big success is just around the corner.

I take a step toward her in time to see Helmut, my main competition, is gonna get there first. My fault for not paying closer attention. Helmut isn't a vamp, but he's a bloodsucker nevertheless. He finds wannabes for girlie shows and escort services. The lowest of the low. I hate his guts, and not only because he makes more than I do. I hate him because he reminds me that we both use people to make a living.

The only hope is that this girl hates Germans addicted to speed, oily blonds with tan leather jackets the same color as their skin. My only hope is that she's got no father figure in her life and has been looking for a guy with a freeway of experience lining his face.

The Kraut reaches in his pocket to pull out his *Helmut Schmidt, Talent Scout* card.

Too late, I get mine ready.

Newbies to Hollywood have watched enough movies to know better, but almost every one of them is naive in at least one respect: if you got no credentials and no contacts, yet still manage to land an agent, it's a safe bet that the agent is either praying for you or preying on you.

Bad agents count on trust and ignorance to make their living, at least I do. Because there's nothing worse than wasting your time lining up a mark only to lose her to an overdose of reality. There's one thing worse; this girl was about to teach me that. So, anyway, Helmut is two steps away from caging the birdie, when —from out of nowhere—some deaf guy peddling sign-language instruction pamphlets, intercepts. The deaf guy hands my girl an envelope and does some fancy hand-job even I can translate as, "Give me all your money."

She looks at him like she knows he's not on the level, but there's gotta be something wrong with an otherwise healthy adult or he wouldn't be doing this crap for a living. She reaches into her jeans pocket and pulls out a fiver.

And that's when I know that this girl is different, that she looks at the world with the wisdom of someone who realizes she is just passing through. Sophistication like that can be worth plenty in my business. Maybe sanitary pads is thinking too low. Maybe she's gonna be breakfast cereal or even headache pills. I can't wait to sign her.

Once I sign a client, I arrange for dental work, and small cosmetic improvements that don't set me back too much. Once I sign a client, she's mine for life. Then it's twenty-five percent plus. The twenty-five percent covers expenses but the plus is what keeps me alive.

For this girl, I'm ready to deal.

I have no choice but to do Rasputin-eyes right there and then. This is something I don't like to show too much of, except for emergencies. If someone—not in my line of vision—was to see me, they might get suspicious. As I am here most every night, suspicion I cannot afford. I prefer blending in. No limelight for me, not my style.

But now I gotta show some tricks or I'll lose her. I make my mind go solid, then send out a mental Valentine just for her.

The girl looks my way, only for a second, but that's all it takes.

I give her *Eyes*. It's an offer she cannot refuse, and I mean really.

Without so much as a glance toward Helmut, she shows her teeth, in a friendly way, and heads toward me.

She's close enough I can smell her. She puts down her carry-on and I'm in heaven cause it looks like she's gonna hug me. "Oh," she says, stepping back. "Sorry. For a second I thought I knew you."

"You do," I tell her. I grasp her hand and give it a firm shake. Her skin is warm, supple. I pick up her carry-on. "I'm your new best friend."

I introduce myself and learn her name is Kyla.

Meanwhile, that Teutonic tarantula is watching my every move. He runs his fingers through his hair and does a bad-Elvis grin. Before I know it, he's all over me, patting my shoulder, squeezing my hand. He ogles my girl with two of his eyes.

I'd feed him to alligators, but that would be cruelty to animals.

"You look familiar," he tells Kyla. "Are you a model?"

The guy's so slick he could slide backwards out of a boa with a bad case of hemorrhoids.

Kyla stares at him, then glances downward. Her cheeks glow pink. She's smart enough to see he's pulling her leg; no doubt it embarrasses her that she's flattered anyway.

She's hungry for attention; that's why she came here. I plan to give her what she needs and more.

"I'd like to be a model," she says, "but I'm not tall enough."

He smiles, thrusts his card at her. "Kismet," he says. "My business is finding models. And you're plenty tall. Maybe not for runway, but certainly for ads. Perhaps movies."

This is where it gets tricky. I like to stay clear of Helmut. He's more of a hustler than I wanna be, so I'll usually give up a mark to avoid a fight.

Not tonight. This girl has made me feel young again.

Better late than never I give her my card. She likes me more than him. I don't kid myself—it's the Rasputin-eyes. "Don't sign anything," I tell her, "until you check with a lawyer about the contract."

"I can't afford a lawyer," she says.

"I can," I say. "I'll pick up the tab."

Helmut's mouth hangs open like a steamed clamshell. "It's his contract you should beware of," he hisses.

"Not a problem," I say. "You pick any lawyer in the phone book. I'll let him draw up a contract."

"You want her that bad, you can keep her," says Helmut.

I am glad that he's in such a generous mood and I can call it a night earlier than usual. I'm hungrier than I should be and afraid that if I don't get a snack I might lose control.

Kyla slips a slender arm beneath mine. "Thanks," she says. "There was something about him I didn't trust—can't say exactly why."

We head toward baggage claim.

My sixth sense lets me feel Helmut's eyes on my back.

*

There's a fair number of vamp-owned businesses in Los Angeles; one is based right here at the airport. A friend started the Night Rider Cab Company. He's got ten drivers working for him now, all good people. Most of them were rescued from the streets, rescued just in time to keep them from going over.

"Evening, Vic," says the youngster, Rudy. He'll be twenty-one for the rest of his days, but he's smart enough not to rub that in. He opens the door and I help Kyla inside, then step around to the other door to let myself in.

Rudy hoists her bags into the trunk and asks, "Where to?"

Before I have a chance to tell him, Kyla blurts out, "Please! Could we drive by Hollywood Boulevard? I know this is silly and it's just concrete, but I've always wanted to see the sidewalk stars."

"Your nickel," says Rudy. By this time I'm famished, not up to sightseeing before dinner. Kyla's looking more delectable by the minute, though I have always drawn the line at snacking on a girl before she's signed. It's poor form.

"Sure," I say. "We'll see the sights, but we gotta stop at the club first. I need to eat."

"The club?" says Kyla.

Rudy tips his hat. "We're on our way."

The club is owned by a blood brother named Barry. He books his talent through me, buys supplies from a vamp food broker at American Grocer. Uses Night Rider for all his transportation needs. Runs a vamp homeless shelter during the day. No matter what you think of us, we've got the networking thing down pat.

Kyla says, "This is all too unbelievable, Victor," and sidles up close enough that I can smell her heart beating beneath a layer of jasmine cologne.

Maybe I went a little heavy on the Rasputin-eyes. Frankly, she's driving me crazy.

"I know the competition is tough," she says, "and I don't have much of a chance, but I've always wanted to be in movies. And not just to be a star or because of the money. I think I could be really good. Make a difference in how people see things."

So she wants to be an artist. I respect that.

"You do theater in your home town?" I ask.

"A little. High school plays. I played Golda in Fiddler on the Roof."

"You? Golda? I'd have cast you as one of the daughters."

"Looks can be deceiving," she says. "I'm a lot older on the inside."

"Me too," I say.

She makes me feel I could say anything, be totally honest about myself without losing her. Not that I am honest with her —I just feel like I could be if I wanted.

We talk and talk and talk; in fifteen minutes it's like I've known her all my life. I wouldn't mind spending more time with her. Been a while since I felt this way. A long while. I put my arm around her shoulder and give her a friendly hug.

She nuzzles her face into my shoulder, says, "I'm not as naive as you might think. I understand that nobody ever does something for nothing."

Her hand rests just above my knee.

"But I want you to know," she says, "that I would sleep with you anyway. You're very attractive," she says. "And funny. That's a rare combination, don't you think?"

Either she's a better actress than I gave her credit for or she means it. If I get a vote, I'd say she means it.

"I'll admit," she says, "that I might not have picked you out of a crowd. Your being a talent agent got my attention. But that's not the only reason why I'm interested in you. I like you. I want you to know that."

I sit there, the tension growing unbearable and for all the wrong reasons. I figure she's still under the influence of Rasputin-eyes; for some reason, that bugs me.

She takes my hand in hers. "About sex," she says. "Don't worry. I won't have regrets. It's okay if that's what you want from me; the feeling is mutual."

"That's not what I want," I tell her. I want something from her, all right, but what I want goes much deeper than sex.

Still, her touch, the fragrance of her blood, the warmth of her leg pressing against mine—it drives me to distraction. I can't take much more.

Contract be damned, I lean over; her scent fills the inside of me. I cup one breast in my hand, thinking of how delicious she will taste, how satisfied I'll feel after. In the back of my mind, a ghostly fear lingers that I'm hungry enough I'll take too much, drain her to the point where she'll have to either go vampire or be forever lost to the world.

It scares me that these are my only choices. I pull back.

"What's wrong?" she asks.

Rudy watches me from the rearview mirror and I can see he's curious as to what I might do. This is not his style; he's usually very discreet, professional.

It's this girl. She's got to him, too. She makes us all do things we wouldn't normally do.

Rudy winks and gives me the thumbs up.

I feel all twisted up inside. It is not altogether unpleasant.

If I wanted I could take her right then, drain her blood, force some of my own back down her throat. Do a vampire wedding ceremony in the back of a taxi with Rudy as the justice of the peace. She'd be mine forever.

Only I can't bring myself to do it.

"Get us to the club," I say, my voice cracking from thirst. "Hurry."

"We're there," says Rudy.

That's when I notice that we've been circling the place, that Rudy has been biding his time, waiting for my signal to let us out.

"Wait here," I say.

Rudy just smiles.

The club is dark and appropriately smoky, which does a pretty good job of covering the smell of blood. A vamp band plays top forty dance tunes. They're even pretty good. The vamp hostess leads us to my usual table at the back. Our vamp waiter shows me the special wine list.

"Would you like a drink?" I ask.

Kyla says, "Diet Pepsi."

I order a glass of the special "RBC Cabernet."

I excuse myself to use the executive restroom. It's all I can do not to run because I'm desperate to use a vampwhore. The owner keeps several desperados on staff, trading them heroin for blood. A good deal all around.

It takes several minutes to drink a cup from a scruffy looking fellow named Buck. I charge it to my account. This kid's blood and the "cabernet" ought to hold me for a couple of hours.

Kyla has ordered the calamari appetizer. "I've always wanted to try these," she says, offering me a breaded tentacle.

She's adorable, and I've never even wanted to try calamari.

I order the Steak Tartare. My waiter winces and pronounces it an excellent choice.

Kyla asks for the filet mignon, well done. "Wanna dance?" she says.

It's a slow number; holding her in my arms leaves me breathless. I'm gonna need another glass of cabernet, that's for sure. Maybe I should just order the bottle. Sometimes it takes another person to make you see you've been lonely.

Kyla strokes my chin and lets her fingers tickle my lips. I almost moan in front of everyone. I nuzzle against her, lick the salt from her neck and prepare to go down, taste what she's really made of. I want to make this girl my life partner, I'm sure of it. And on the first date no less.

I open my mouth, run my tongue along her skin, scrape my teeth over her collarbone, and sink them into her. She tastes sweet, warm. I can't get enough. I hold her and suckle at her neck, feeling her body relax as she gives herself over to me. She's mine, she will always be mine. Not that she ever had a choice.

My Rasputin-eyes made certain of that. It hits me then, what I'm doing, and I'm overcome with shame for wanting to use her. I pull away. Some scruples I got. She deserves more.

I got a crushing feeling in my chest, like the first time I woke up in a coffin. There are roads you never wanna walk down because once you do, the next thing you know, you find yourself supplying girls to escort joints, hitting on every Joe you take a fancy to without caring whether or not that kills him.

I've seen this happen too many times, had to stand by helplessly as Lucy, my ex, lost that last drop of humanity just before she went over. Once you lose respect for them you lose respect for yourself.

No way will I let that happen to me.

Kyla flashes a smile so slight it seems painted on. "Are you okay? Sorry if I'm pushing things." She looks worried. "It's just that sometimes you wait too long and you never get the chance again."

"No problem." I say, knowing exactly what she means. Opportunity is knocking, only I know better than to open the door. I feel sick. It's not hunger, but the terrifying realization that I am stark-raving-lunatic in love with this girl. Worse, I want her to love me back, to choose me the way I have chosen her. I won't coerce her into the life like Lucy did to me.

It ain't real love when it's forced, and if it ain't real, what's the point of pretending? Hollywood or not, it ain't for me.

We walk back to our table, neither one speaking. The hair at the back of my neck bristles. Helmut is sitting at the bar, watching us. He's drinking something with milk in it and lifts his glass, mouthing, "Cheers." So he's followed me here, the little prick. Suddenly, I want to run away, but there's no running away and seeing Helmut just reminds me of that.

He stands then, wobbling just a little, makes his way to our table. His eyes fix on Kyla's tits like he's staring into her eyes. "You're making a big mistake," he says. "If it's still not too late, I'd like you to reconsider my offer."

"Maybe you should reconsider," I say. I'm scared to lose her but even more scared she'll stay. "You got anything legit to offer?" I ask him.

Helmut grins. "Of course," he says. "There's always jobs for those who want the work."

Kyla crosses her arms, shrugs. "Sorry," she says. "I'm happy where I am."

Helmut does not take this well. He points his finger at her, says, "You don't have what it takes and I can tell. I wasn't always a troll. I used to be somebody, work with real talent. Ask this guy if he's sent any clients to the big time? He's no better than me, only he won't admit it. Don't say I didn't warn you." He staggers back to the bar.

I'm surprised to learn he's jealous. So Helmut wants what I got. How can I tell him it ain't worth all that much?

Kyla holds her head up straight. She tries to look into my eyes, but breaks away. "Is that true?" she asks.

"It's true," I admit.

She wants me to tell her she's got everything, more than everything, that there's never been another girl like her.

But I'll never get rid of her if I tell her the truth. Funny thing is, I'll never get rid of her no matter what I tell her. "You're a nice girl," I say, "but there's nothing special about you."

She excuses herself to use the bathroom. I see her shoulders tense up like she's sobbing.

It takes all I have not to go after her.

Meanwhile, a vamp waitress is looking at Helmut like she's never seen anything like him.

He returns her stare, and for a minute I wonder who is scamming who?

I got a feeling that before the evening is done, Helmut will become a vamp or else he'll be dead.

I don't want to stay around to see which way it goes.

I tell our waiter to doggie-bag our orders to go. "We gotta get out of here," I say when Kyla comes back.

She gives me the silent treatment, probably better that way.

If I had a heart it would be breaking.

Rudy hauls us back to the airport. If it took an hour drive here it now takes three hours to ride back. Before we get out, I empty my wallet into Kyla's hand.

She stares at the money, already hurting too much to be insulted.

"It just ain't happening here," I say. "It will never happen here. Sorry."

At the counter I charge her ticket to my card.

She clears her throat. "Victor," she begins.

"Stop," I say. I do Rasputin-eyes and whisper that she's to go home, forget all about me, find somebody else, somebody who deserves her. "You don't want what I have to give," is the last thing I say. Her plane won't leave till morning. I still got one more choice to make. Sooner or later, everyone goes over. I know that all too well.

The question is, do I hang around and watch Kyla's plane take off? Or save up my goodbyes for another day?

WHY A DUCK

First appeared in *Zeppelin Adventure Stories,*
Wheatland Press, 2004

Ten minutes into the race, the pilot of the pink "Last Gas"
went about his duties, unaware that he was carrying
two ghosts as stowaways. One of the ghosts, Anthony, stood
in the center of the gondola and looked out. Hot-air balloons
hissed like unruly geese competing for the forward point in the
formation. The only barriers between here and eternity were
the fog-shrouded mountains, the colorful balloons being blown
across the sky like a spray of opaque bubbles, and a banner of
pastel clouds. The view was spectacular: a circle in the round
theater, except without any nausea. The balloon passed through
a pocket of dead air; they hovered momentarily. A swirl of leaves
stopped moving through the sky and was held in one place like
pressed flowers between planes of wind. "Beautiful," Anthony
said to his wife, the other ghost.

"Yes, dear," Beatrice answered.

Anthony was dressed in the same hospital gown he had died
in. Barefoot, except the toe tag. Obeying his mother's lessons by
wearing new Fruit-Of-The-Loom in case of accident had proved
an exercise in futility. The nurses had found it necessary to cut
off his briefs in the emergency room, then incinerated his bloody
clothing—without leaving so much as a single notation on the
medical chart about the condition of his personal effects. Nobody
would ever learn about the condition of his underwear, which
had probably ended up in a rag bin in Ohio. Good thing the dead

did not require underwear at all, or he'd be in big trouble. A cool gust of wind parted his gown and smacked his butt cheeks. He found the sensation refreshing.

Anthony lived for flying; his balloon was cruising above three thousand feet. He knew it was his imagination but he could smell the earthy odor of the potato fields below. The ground gave off a pleasant scent, like clean dirt and the wings of sun-warmed beetles. An eddy of wind forced them downward and for a moment the peppermint pink-striped envelope went slack before it straightened out and lifted the balloon back into position.

"Whee!" cried Anthony. Uncertainty was all part of the fun.

Beatrice shivered. She squeezed into Anthony's space in front of the burners.

He liked having her so near but could sense her pushing him away. He floated backwards.

"I'm cold," she said, and thrust her translucent hands into the flames; her skin took on the elegant appearance of candied orange peel.

Though Anthony had nothing to compare her to, he thought she made for a most attractive ghost. She was DOA when their balloon crashed, so she was still wearing her red jogging suit with a white stripe down the pants, and clean white sneakers. Too bad she had not died in something lacy and crotchless, but oh well. As it happened, she matched the balloon rather nicely. She was a lovely woman, even in nylon, even six months dead.

He did his best to puff out his chest and hoped he still looked good to her. He was not terribly vain, a good thing, as vanity was something of a wasted conceit once a man had died.

The balloon dipped again, and the pilot, a man in a funny little cap dumped some ballast and moved in from the edge to check his cables. The pilot tightened a screw on the load rings and gave a couple of twists to the nozzle to release more hot air into the envelope. He said, "That ought to do it," without an indication that he believed anyone was there to hear him. When most people talked, they were only talking to themselves anyway. This man was no different.

The pilot wanted to breakaway from the middle of the pack and fly out front, where he could lay claim upon the sky. His cap was the style of an old railroad cap, made from pink silk, a slightly lighter shade than the balloon.

Anthony wondered if the man was queer; crossing the sky in a hot air balloon could make a man do crazy things, as Anthony knew too well. Beatrice seemed to think he'd been crazy for a long time; she had never shared his passion for ballooning, and barely tolerated his hobby. Anthony sighed. This was more than a hobby; it was a way of life. At least, it had been. When you thought about it, they didn't really have much in common. Especially if you didn't count those fifty years and seven children.

And now, of course, this.

"I'm cold," Beatrice said.

She was always cold. Anthony suspected some problem with her metabolism. There had to be an explanation for why she still felt cold even in sweat pants, while he was practically naked and yet cozy as ever.

"Do you want my..." he started before remembering he had no coat. It wouldn't do to give her his gown, not that he would mind the sacrifice. He wasn't so sure he could manage undoing the straps in any event. He and Beatrice were mirror opposites in so many ways... for one thing, Beatrice would not want to spend eternity seeing him naked.

She was hugging herself and he moved close to wrap his arms around her but there was nothing to hold onto and his hands passed right through her.

Neither one of them was all there; you couldn't hug an illusion. "We need more mass," he said.

She gave him a funny look. "Like that would help any," she said.

"It couldn't hurt," he said.

"You and your harebrained schemes," she said. "Why do you

think we're here in the first place?"

"Don't start," he warned. There was only so much blame for things that a man could accept. Whenever you took chances, things could happen. Even when you stood in one place, you couldn't be so sure that you would be safe. That was the nature of reality—their lives were not under personal control. Sure, ballooning was an obsession, a disease, like alcoholism, and perhaps just as often fatal. Anthony did not care at all about statistics.

Who would want to take root in the middle of a potato farm when he could soar above eagles? Who would want to mow the lawn if he could be in the hangar stuffing sandbags?

"If you think back, you'll remember that I warned you there was a cold front coming!" she said. "I told you we shouldn't go up in those conditions."

He was about to rehash their argument when he grew dizzy and the colors inside the basket began to swirl like colorful clay atop a potter's wheel being shaped into a bowl. He could no longer hold himself upright; he pitched backward.

"Not again," he said. This was the downside of the death experience. They existed in scenes that faded in and out as their balloon drifted out of range of their haunt zone. The scene was almost over.

"Shit!" Beatrice screamed. It was so unlike her to curse. "Here it comes! I hate this part. How could you do this to me? You know I don't like surprises!" She may have continued on with her rant, but he did not hear her.

When he recovered consciousness, they were in another balloon; this one checkered and brown with a new pilot. This pilot was dressed in army fatigues and wore thick black boots. Anthony gazed over at the compass and noted that they were in the same starting place as before. Below them, the potato fields resembled a spotted green and brown blanket that had gone through the wash a few too many times to look pristine. Familiar and comfortable—even if junky—the kind of thing you loved yet put away when guests stopped by.

A feeling of emptiness overcame him. Anthony whipped around and felt a sense of relief course through him when he spotted Beatrice hugging the burners. Not that Beatrice could have gone anywhere without him, but he craved reassurance, needed to be certain that she was still there.

"You okay?" he asked.

"It's cold," she said. She squinted and said, "Why couldn't we be planted in a field like normal people? Why couldn't we be out haunting a house and scaring the cats and saying normal things, like, 'Boo!'?"

"I don't know," he said. "Maybe nobody stays down there after they die. Maybe 'normal' is what you make of it." He didn't believe that. He believed that they were up here because he had wanted to be up here, because he hadn't been ready to give up his dream, settle down, take root like an old potato. And she hadn't been strong enough in her convictions to overturn his.

It must have been difficult, being a woman of her time. After the children left home, Beatrice had never really found herself. If anyone had ever needed a hobby, it was her.

The pilot opened a hinged box and got out a plastic mask. He was about the age that Anthony had been, before the accident. Old. Ancient. Wrinkled. The age at which, when you smiled at a young lady, she assumed that you were only being polite instead of horny. The pilot took a hit off his oxygen mask and smiled at the expanse of sky.

"Lightweight," said Anthony. They weren't even at 4000 feet. He beat his chest and pretended to gulp in the air. Plenty of oxygen! Who needed drugs?

"Eternity is so, well, so boring," Beatrice said. "Look at this!" She pointed down to the potato fields and at a couple of turkey vultures circling to the north in preparation for descent. "I deserve more. I want angels! I want heavenly harps!"

"I'm sorry," Anthony said. "This is all I can give you." It irritated him that this wasn't enough. After all this time, he didn't understand her. Why did she always want more than he offered? What was it with women, anyway?

"I'm cold," Beatrice said. "I don't like being surrounded by so much air. I want to be wrapped up, buried under ground where the wind won't touch me."

That sounded horrible; coffins were so confining. Not wanting to argue, Anthony said nothing. He felt a little guilty for making her miserable and hoped the fade would come quickly and they could get out of this scene. Maybe in the next one, they wouldn't fight.

Unfortunately, they were caught in a tailwind and the balloon drifted back the way they had come. At this rate, they would never advance. Fades only happened when they went the distance. It didn't matter how long it took for them to get there.

The pilot took another hit of oxygen and flashed a stoner smile at the sky. Anthony tried to will him to dump ballast or steer them out of here, but his ethereal presence didn't register a blip on the pilot's radar. This pilot didn't care about winning or being *Number One* in this race. Anthony disliked the man. They weren't going anywhere and the pilot was taking them there.

"Why do men want balloons, anyway?" Beatrice asked.

He shrugged. It seemed too obvious to explain.

"Weren't the children enough? What about your job? And me? Why did you need more than that?"

"Look around you," he said. "Isn't this glorious?"

"Glory, schmory," she said. "If I wanted glory I would have died at the Macy's after-Christmas sale."

"I hardly think you can compare the experience of mark-down linens with this," Anthony said.

"Shopping has a point! A beginning and an end! With balloons, you just float around and never go anywhere."

"You do too."

"Do not! When you land, a crew hauls you back to your car. How is that going anywhere?"

"Think of it this way. We're having an adventure."

"This isn't an adventure!" she said. "It's play acting adventure. In real adventure you get sharks!"

He was tired of fighting with her and wanted it to end. They would rehash this same argument forever if he didn't do something to change their course! "That's it!" he said. "The last straw. You want real adventure? I'll give you something to remember!" He felt emboldened and floated up to the basket rim. There, he teetered on the edge. He held out his hands in Superman position. "I'll jump!" he said. "If you say another word, that's what I'll do!"

"Oh, please," said Beatrice. Her teeth were chattering without making any noise. "You're not the jumping type."

"I'll jump! I really will!" he said. He leaned into the wind and let the currents hold him aloft. "Here I go!"

"You're afraid," she said. "You won't really do it."

That's where she was wrong. He pushed off, arching his back in his best approximation of a swan dive. But he didn't fall. To fall, you had to weigh something. He was like the air inside of a cookie cutter. All outline. No substance. The chagrin!

"I told *you* you couldn't do it!" Beatrice said. She made a tsk-tsking sound. "Now get back in this balloon before the scene fades!"

"I don't think so," Anthony told her. He still wanted to jump. More than ever, in fact.

She frowned and wrinkles formed and made her face look like a balloon before it was fully inflated. "Anthony, please," she said. She wrung her hands. "What will happen when we fade if you're out there and I'm in here?" She sounded worried.

He wanted to test their relationship. "Then come out here and be with me," he said.

She shook her head and did not look convinced. "I should have married Burt Pinkerton," she said. "He was a banker, had his feet on the ground."

"I remember Burt Pinkerton," Anthony said. "He had dandruff and a black mole on his upper lip."

"Well, besides that," she said, as she moved toward the edge of the balloon. She reached for him.

Out of habit, he grasped her hand to help her out of the gondola. Now, for the first time, he could feel her. "Oh wow," he said, her small ghostly hand fitting snugly in his slightly larger one. "You don't know how nice this feels."

She smiled with coyness he still found charming. "I know," she said. "I know."

A flock of wood ducks approached in classic "V" formation, their feathers iridescent as balloon skins. "I have an idea," Anthony said. He let go of her hand and turned away from her. "Quick! Wrap your legs around my waist, like I'm giving you a piggy back ride."

"What! Anthony Wilson, are you crazy?"

"No. As sane as I ever was! Trust me. This will work."

"Oh, for heaven's sake," she said, but climbed atop his back as he suggested.

He could feel her light-as-air, cool body pressed against him. Her arms snuggled kudzu-like around his neck. If he had been alive, she would have choked him. Being dead, he rather enjoyed the extra stimulation. With Beatrice hugging him, he felt almost whole. "Here's what to do: the second the ducks fly by, grab them. Use their mass to carry us away."

"This is ridiculous," she said.

"I don't think so. It's science."

"What kind of science uses ducks?" she asked.

"There's no time to argue," he insisted. This was true.

As the ducks passed over them, he reached up toward the forest of scaly feet and managed to snag two ducks. He gripped one twig-like leg in each hand and felt the webbed feet tense beneath his palms. It was working! Alone, each ghost was nothing; together they were something. The ducks could not ignore them.

His fingers curling around the duck feet must have tickled like spider webs; the ducks tried to shake him off in order to rejoin their group.

"Boo," Anthony said as the ducks quacked and complained. He turned his chin toward Beatrice, "See! It works."

Beatrice had not let go of his neck in time to grab for a duck of her own. "Sorry," she said. "They were too fast for me."

"It will be okay," he said. "We'll share. Take one of my ducks."

"I'm afraid," she said. "I don't want to let go."

"Squeeze me tighter with your legs," he said. "You won't fall."

"Oh, Anthony!" she said.

"We'll make it work with only the two ducks between us. I've done the calculations. Go ahead and grab one of mine. Take hold of one foot in each hand and let it carry your weight, not that you have much."

"I'm not sure about this," she said. He could feel the pressure of her elbow squeezing his temple as she reached up to grip the duck by its leg. She was terrified but knew how to be brave.

"Perfect," he said. "Now the other hand."

"I'm afraid."

"It will be all right," he said. "Trust me."

"I do trust you," she said. She let go of his neck and blindly grabbed for the other leg. He could tell that she was scared by the way her feet dug into his belly.

When he felt her grip was secure, he let go of her duck and concentrated on steering his. The duck was uncooperative and twisted its neck and wiggled its tail as it tried to shake him off. They dipped, sped up, ascended, then plummeted, and having no ballast, could not control their rapid descent. Wind whipped up his hospital gown like a flag at half-mast in the middle of a hurricane.

"Whee! This is great!" Anthony said. He had never felt such exhilaration. They continued to accelerate as they approached the ground. "Isn't this wonderful?" he asked.

She was screaming too hard to answer. Disoriented, she let go of her duck and it flew away, squawking.

He couldn't blame her. It was her first skydive. His too, without a parachute.

His duck tried a new tactic to be rid of them and flew around in circles.

"Sorry," Beatrice said. "I don't think one duck will be enough to get us very far."

"We'll make do," Anthony told her. "One duck is more than most people get."

"Can I, maybe, hold yours?" she said.

"Any time," he said. "You don't even need to ask."

"I want to kiss you," she said, and she carefully climbed around to face him, never quite letting go of him. She wrapped her legs around his hips and pressed her cold chest against his to snuggle. One arm gripped his neck as the other flew up to grip the duck's leg at its ankle. She brought her icy lips to his and said, "I love you." Then, she started to let go, first with her hand as she reached up toward the duck. She said, "Here goes nothing," and dropped both legs from his waist. The two of them dangled, facing each other, while the duck carried them through the sky.

"Whee," Beatrice said.

Anthony felt the tickle from the duck's webbed foot as it struggled to escape. "Are you still cold?" he asked.

"Who cares about the weather?" she said. Her voice was more animated than usual.

They were off-balance and started to spin. With her facing him, Anthony could not control his duck with any degree of precision. The duck, being a duck, did as it wanted, which was try to shake them off. Soon, they were all tumbling and falling through the air as both duck and human pilots struggled to steer the craft. The potato fields were below them while at the same time above them or beside them. Thrill and terror coursed through him.

"Whee!" Anthony said.

He felt lightheaded and watched a world pass by him in fast-forward. "Hold me!" he shrieked. "Don't ever let me go!"

"Okay," she whispered in his ear. He felt the warmth and moisture of her breath and a comforting pressure as she again slid her legs around his waist.

"I must confess I rather like that," he said.

"Screw the duck," she said, letting go so she could wrap her arms around his neck and smother his lips with hers.

Distracted, he forgot what he was doing and in that split-second when his mind was elsewhere, the duck slipped away.

"I love you," he said.

"Me too," she answered.

Without warning, the scene faded. When he came to, Beatrice was still humping him but they were in a new gondola piloted by a man who was having some trouble lighting his pipe.

Anthony sighed. "Thank God, we didn't end up in a potato field," he said, hoping it wasn't the wrong thing to say after their adventure, that it wouldn't get her started again.

Beatrice smiled up at him. "I love you," she said.

"Me too," he answered.

The pilot drew on the pipe and finally managed to get the tobacco started.

Beatrice reached out with one hand to extinguish the fire.

The pilot looked alarmed.

"Tee hee!" Beatrice cried. She pointed upward. A lone duck flew way behind his flock as it tried to catch up. "Look, Anthony! There goes one. Can we do it again?"

"I think so," he said. "In fact, I'm sure of it." He was clam-happy. This was everything he'd ever wanted. Maybe more. Too bad it hadn't all happened earlier; thank goodness, it wasn't too late now.

"I have an idea," Anthony said.

"Tell me," said Beatrice.

Anthony gulped in air, then shouted, "Boo!" and managed to keep from laughing. "Boo!" Anthony shouted again, checking to see if the pilot so much as flinched.

MY HERMIT

First appeared in *Mota: Courage*,
Tripletree Publications, 2004

My name is Theodora Lansing and I am the chair of Hermit Studies at the University of Oregon. My interest in Hermit Studies is related to my unusual family history. My father was a hermit, as was his father, and his father's father, and his father's father's father before him. On the maternal side, my mother and her mother, and her mother's mother, and her mother's mother's mother before her were all raised in single-parent households, as was I. The consistency of my family's phenotype is atypical. My familial contacts and sociological research suggests that the traits, attitudes, and lifestyles associated with hermits are genetic in origin (a recessive sex-linked allele on the X chromosome) and not a psychosocial trait as was previously believed.

Students often ask me how it happens that hermits who relish isolation manage to reproduce with such regularity. It only takes one night and two hermits, as we say in the field.

Hermit Studies at the U of O is an interdisciplinary study, and my doctorate was in Sociology, one of the so-called soft sciences. My dissertation had focused on alternative familial groupings, and my book, The Hermit's Way had become the standard in the field. Our faculty included the Jungian research psychologist Brittany Lake, and an overreaching geneticist named Daniel Nathaniel Rickman.

We met weekly in the windowless faculty lounge in the basement of the Humanities building. The current discussion concerned the upcoming Fall Colloquium, which we were calling "Hikikomori (the Japanese term for Hermit Syndrome, meaning to shut oneself inside) in the Post-Industrial World." Rickman initiated a long and pointless discussion on whom to invite as the keynote speaker. Rickman favored J. D. Salinger, while Lake favored Pynchon. Not being one for speeches, I didn't care. We tabled the discussion and moved on to new business.

I brought up something that had been bothering me. "This may seem trivial," I began, unable to meet my colleagues' eyes. "But someone has been eating my yogurt."

There was an uncomfortable quiet that was either a guilty silence or the silence of those trying not to laugh. Shopping was not a pleasant experience. I wasn't a people person; I limited interactions whenever possible. Perhaps the thief would now think twice before ransacking the department refrigerator.

The hermit male is seldom found at recitals or Little League games or school open houses. Hermit males, as one might expect, prefer to live alone, often in geographic isolation, and often in habitats consisting of one room, lacking the most primitive plumbing and electricity. Hermit males typically cook meals out of one pot and use a large bowl and spoon as primary eating utensils. The personal habits of hermit males are much debated, but contrary to popular myth, hermits pay close attention to cleanliness and grooming. A hermit's life is not chaotic but highly structured. It is, perhaps, this desire for structure that leads the hermit away from the unpredictable demands of modern civilization.

—*The Hermit's Way*, by Theodora Lansing

My mother was a bus driver who had worked for the Lane County Transit District since I was an infant. There were two kinds of bus drivers: the chatty ones who made eye contact with everyone on their route and knew before you did that it was time to pull the cord and get off. My mother was the other kind, the seemingly rude bus driver who discouraged conversation. She failed to anticipate her customers' needs and was frequently caught off-guard when riders waited a split-second too long to signal their intentions. Even though the same people rode her route day in and day out, there were few she knew by name, despite many reminders. She was a dreadful and abrupt driver. If my mother hadn't had the union equivalent of tenure, I don't know how she would have kept her job.

In an act that surprised me for its unselfishness, my mother had begrudgingly allowed me to scrape cells from inside her cheek. With Rickman's assistance, I had examined her DNA, stared at her genetic markers with the intensity of a mother staring at her newborn, but I did not really know her on a deeper level. I regretted but could do nothing about that. My mother had provided for me physically and financially; she did not know how to encourage the emotional growth of a child.

Wednesdays, I rode her bus to campus, the best way I had found to see her on a regular basis, even if the route was a bit out of my way. I drove to a neighborhood in West Eugene near my mother's first stop, parked, got out my umbrella and briefcase, and locked the car. I waited at the stop, grateful that my communion with the foggy May Oregon morning was limited to a few minutes because my mother was Greenwich time-punctual. I waved wildly as her bus approached, standing on my tiptoes to make sure that she'd see me and stop to let me on. She always stopped; it was just that she never slowed to give warning. Her inability to signal her intent when dealing with others seemed pathological.

Money ready, I closed my umbrella and shook off the rain before boarding. I tried to catch her glance, to have her acknowledge my presence. My glasses fogged, so I couldn't see if she smiled. "Hi, Mom," I said and paid the fare.

She gunned it, causing me to fall into the first empty seat. Nobody else was there to see my clumsy entrance, not that I cared. "How are you?" I asked.

"I won a hundred dollars at bingo last night," she said, and honked the horn to warn the car ahead of her that it was traveling too slowly. The car moved into the left lane to let her pass on its right.

"Hey! Congratulations," I said. "Are you going to buy yourself something nice?"

She shrugged and gave me a blank stare in the rearview mirror. I had the feeling I'd gotten too personal. I asked about her cat.

"He's fine," she said. She roared along, seemingly oblivious of the woman half a block up on the right who was decked out in a fluorescent orange rain suit and jumping up and down like a cheerleader.

I knew better than to say anything, but grabbed hold of the seat in preparation for the inevitable stop.

Mom hit the brakes and my briefcase slid to the front.

The woman in the rain suit hopped on, flashed her bus pass, and said with sincerity, "Thanks for stopping." She picked up my briefcase and looked at me. "This yours?" she asked, as she took a step back. My mother pulled away from the curb and the woman in the rain suit tumbled into the seat beside me. "I just moved to Eugene," she said, and told me that her name was Miriam. In the next breath I learned that she was recently divorced, had a daughter in kindergarten, and that her mother watched the child while Miriam attended the University.

I longed for this type of arrangement.

"What's your major?" I asked, to be polite, hoping that she wouldn't answer sociology because I didn't care to fraternize with my students.

"Early childhood education," she said. "I really want to understand about my kid."

The bus choked to a stop and in the eerie still I heard my mother's stomach growl.

"Do your parents live in town?" Miriam asked.

Not knowing if my mother was listening to our conversation

182

MY HERMIT

or not, I answered yes. I disliked this sort of personal grilling and turned to stare out the window, but Miriam wasn't adept at picking up on my social cues.

"You're so lucky," Miriam said. "I wish I'd never moved away from my mother in the first place. Are you guys close?"

My mouth went dry and I tried to smile, but my face felt so numb I feared that I was grimacing. I pointed to the woman who gripped the steering wheel as if it were the only thing that kept her anchored to her seat. "That's my mom," I said.

"Oh," said Miriam. "How nice."

Typically, the offspring of hermits do not get to know their fathers. This was my own experience—and very likely one of the primary forces shaping my life and choice of profession. One of the benefits of being an academic was that I understood my father's behavior the way a scientist understands her subject, instead of looking at my father as a child typically views her parent. Once each summer, in early June, I made the pilgrimage to Eastern Oregon to visit the man who was my biological father.

As the crow flew, my father only lived about one hundred miles away. Not being a crow, my journey took much longer. The trip was a scenic drive across the Cascades. My father had built his isolated cabin in a wilderness in the shadow of Mt. Bachelor. It was a lovely spot—exactly the kind of place a person might choose if he wanted to get away from it all.

Which obviously, my father did.

I parked in a Forest Service lot, tightened my hiking bootlaces, readied my backpack frame, and began the rather difficult hike along a seldom-used wilderness trail. I wore a sun hat, long pants, and a long-sleeved cotton shirt, despite its being in the high nineties, for we were in the midst of an unusual hot spell. The sun could only scorch the surface, but bugs and snakes could get inside this skin. Long sleeves made me feel less vulnerable. My pack held enough supplies to last through the first two weeks at the end of the world, plus a homemade lemon Bundt cake for my

183

dad.

I wore a combination pedometer and compass to help me keep track of my route. I headed east, into the sun. The hills provided an off-key orchestration of bird calls and cicada wings and crackling twigs and chattering squirrels. Not being much of an outdoorswoman, I tired after a couple of hours and stopped to rest at my favorite granite rock in the center of a spooky stand of dead lodgepole pine.

It was like hiking into a Hemingway story; everything was sepia-toned and bristling with subtext. Slender lodgepole pine corpses jutted from the ground like broken bones. The native flora had long ago burned and been replaced by spotted knapweed that bloomed with alien-looking purple-thorn flowers and choked the ground with an army of green foliage. The rock was porous and sun-warmed, with a flat edge big enough to seat two. I closed my eyes and tried to imagine a cool morning, without success. The horseflies were loud and aggressive, the air heavy with a pungent scent of sun-baked caterpillars and pollen.

I drank bottled water, ate a granola bar, shook the rocks out of my boots, and applied moleskin to my blistered heels. I peed behind the rock and shouldered my pack before going on.

I spotted the basalt outcropping in time to step from the trail, endured another few rocky miles at a four percent incline, and finally found myself back on an abandoned Forest Service path. To the north, I saw Mt. Bachelor. By now it was late afternoon and I felt exhausted. I hiked another 1.7 miles into the back, back, back country. There, in a cluster of Doug fir, I saw my father's house.

He didn't like to be surprised, and even though I visited every year around the same time and had written to him C/O General Mail Call to tell him to expect me yet again, when I came within two hundred feet of the cabin, I called out, "Are you home?" and made my way slowly toward the door.

"Is that you, Theodora?" he asked and it made me laugh, because who else would made this trek to say hello?

"Yes, it's me," I said.

The screen door screeched open and a dark-haired man with a full beard who looked a lot younger than sixty walked out on the porch. He was wearing shorts and a white tee shirt; his upper body was lumberjack-strong. He smiled, and in his smile I saw a look that conveyed both joy and suspicion.

I was thirty-four and he still wasn't used to me. I knew on an intellectual level not to take it personally. I walked close and took off my pack so he could give me a hug, or more precisely, so I could hug him. I held onto him as long as he allowed it. "Nice to see you," I said.

"Thank you for visiting," he said. He picked up my pack and hoisted it over one shoulder. "Would you like to come in?"

I followed him up the steps; he held open the door. His cabin was tidy but snug, divided into sections with throw rugs that marked the perimeters of the kitchen, living, and sleeping areas. The screened windows were open and the tall trees provided enough shade to keep the place cool. He lit the stove and set the kettle over the burners. "Coffee?" he asked.

"Oh!" I said, and went to unpack. "I brought some for you." I dug through my stuff and brought out the coffee and cake. I'd brought filters, too, and handed everything over. The kettle whistled and he poured our coffee into a blue enamel pot. It happened too quickly; it always seemed like water boiled faster out here than back in town.

He brought out a step stool for me to sit at a tiny table and drink. He stayed standing and broke off a piece of cake and took a bite. He offered some to me. I shook my head because this was a present meant for him.

"Good," he said, nodding at the cake.

"I baked it," I said.

He grunted and licked his fingers. "I like the coffee, too," he said, looking acutely uncomfortable, like a man who hoped the encyclopedia salesman would finish his pitch and move on to the neighbors'.

I told him about my research and about my house and about my car. "How are you?" I asked, and he looked out the screened window at the trees and said, "Fine, thank you."

"How are you feeling? Did you get my letters?" I asked, but he just shrugged. I stared at my father, wishing he were capable of loving me.

"Don't you want to know about Mom?" I asked to change the subject. "Last month she won a hundred dollars at bingo."

He gulped down the rest of his coffee and stood. "I'm going to take a walk," he said, and left me, not returning until well past dark, by which time I had already made up my bed beside the hearth.

The hermit pedigree is a fascinating diagram. Males who inherit one affected X-chromosome exhibit a phenotype consistent with full-blown Hikikomori, or hermit syndrome (h-XY). Women with just one affected X chromosome are carriers (h- XX), who frequently exhibit hermit characteristics such as anxiety during enforced social interaction and a lack of empathy toward others. Females with two affected X chromosomes exhibit the typical patterning and behavior associated with the hermit lifestyle (hh XX), however their reclusive behavior can be mitigated by the female's maternal instinct and need for socialization.

Rarely, a Hikikomori female will possess three X chromosomes. In these cases, the Lyon hypothesis of X inactivation occurs (hhH XXx), and it becomes possible for an affected female to mate with a hermit and produce female offspring with only one activated gene (Hh xY). This female will be carrier caught in a peculiar sociological conundrum. Unlike her mother, she will want to experience love and affection. Should the offspring be a male, the cycle of hermit syndrome will be ended.

When the hermit male reproduces, he passes on his affected X chromosome to any daughters (unknown + h XX). Although one might surmise that his healthy Y-chromosome would save future sons from suffering the disorder, his tendency to mate with hermit females or carriers stacks the deck that any offspring will carry or exhibit Hikikomori (unknown + - XY). Thus, the hermit's lineage is assured.

—*The Hermit's Way*, by Theodora Lansing

In late July my mother suffered a heart attack. I didn't learn of it for almost a week, when I took my usual Wednesday bus ride and asked the replacement driver what had happened.

"Oh," said that woman, who was five minutes late to pick me up. "She's in intensive care."

I called the department and left a message for Rickman, asking him to let my teaching assistant know I'd been delayed, subtly hinting that he could help me out of a tight spot and have a look at my assistant's research notes to let her know if she was on the right track. I got off at the next stop and ran back to my car. I drove across town and parked illegally in the doctors' lot. A volunteer directed me toward the Coronary Care Unit waiting room. I signed in to see my mother and sat in a small room that seemed moist from all the tears.

I waited some twenty minutes before knocking on a sliding glass window that protected the receptionist from worried visitors. "Excuse me," I said, and asked to see my mother.

"I'm sorry," the receptionist said. "Only family members are allowed in the unit."

"I am family!" I said. "I'm her daughter!"

"I'm sorry," the receptionist said, giving me the cold look favored by hospital personnel. "You can see her when she's transferred to the step-down unit."

"But I'm family!" I said. "I'm sure she'd want to see me. Please tell her I'm here."

The receptionist checked over her paperwork without bothering to meet my gaze. "I'm sorry," she said. "On her admissions form, your mother marked the box that said she had no living relatives." And with that, she closed her window to leave me stranded on the other side.

The storm front had moved in faster than predicted and there was a steady drizzle when I parked in my usual Forest Service lot. There hadn't been time to warn my father I was coming. Perhaps some part of me still held hope that he would go against nature, move to civilization, and care for mother.

I got into my rain gear and used a plastic garbage bag to cover my pack, anxious to get to my father's cabin before the storm hit full force. The ground was cement hard and steaming with retained heat from the day. I drank in the most wonderful scent of moist pine and wild berries. Rain gear proved to be a miscalculation, as the warmth beneath the rain, combined with the effort of a steady climb left me drenched in sticky sweat. I vowed to shed the protective layers at my usual resting rock in the stand of lodgepole pine. It was the kind of weather where hiking naked made more sense than being clothed.

I kept up a steady pace and surprised myself when, well after over an hour of walking, I hadn't yet reached the lodgepole stand. The air was liquid but my mouth was parched. I didn't drink because I didn't want to have to stop to go to the bathroom. The ground was slippery, muddy in spots, and the sky increasingly dark. My glasses were shower door-foggy and I realized I had lost the path. When I checked my compass, I saw that I was heading south; without the path or familiar markers to aid me in my course, I was unsure how to adjust. I found a relatively dry spot beneath the boughs of a Doug fir, where I took off my pack and rooted through the compartments for my phone. I couldn't get a signal, even when I moved away from the tree.

I simultaneously pushed back panic and let myself be taken in by visions of rising waters and landslides and bones breaking through skin. Bugs feasting on flesh. I remembered everything I'd ever read about hikers who were lost in the woods – hikers eaten by bears or found years later, dead of exposure – and considered whether the odds for survival improved if I ditched my pack, or if refusing to abandon my meager supplies gave me an edge. Being a practical person, I also considered my father's displeasure if I survived this setback and showed up at his cabin without cake. I decided to shoulder the pack.

Because of the clouds, I couldn't use the mountain peaks as markers, but the next time I checked the compass, I was heading due west. If I hit the Deschutes River, that would mean I'd gone too far. I wasn't afraid, just frustrated, and decided to hike for another hour and make camp if I was still unsure of my direction. It had always seemed so odd to me, how wildlife disappeared during a rainstorm. Engineers had designed umbrellas and Gore-Tex and windshield wipers that allowed us navigate through rain, but nature sought shelter through the storm. There was a quiet that I found disconcerting. The mud was tacky brown mountain clay that filled the tread of my boots and left the soles so smooth I skated along the ground. I found myself headed uphill, the walk increasingly treacherous.

I slipped and hit my head against a rock and felt so dizzy, I couldn't stand up for several minutes. I threw up. Despair filled me like mud and I felt shaky, like I was coming down with the flu. I stood and tried to backtrack, limping downhill.

I noticed a single black tendril of smoke rising from a stand of fir. I headed into the woods and spotted a rustic cabin. I made it as far as the stoop before fainting.

When I came to I was snuggled on a mat, my wet things replaced by a quilt stuffed with equal parts of down and musk. A fire roared in the heart and the sweet smell of pine and smoke filled the tiny cabin.

"You okay?" asked a man.

Without my glasses, I could barely make out his features. It hurt to move the parts of my head, but I said, "Yes." I asked him for my glasses and he came close and handed them to me. He looked to be in his mid-forties.

"What are you doing out here?" asked the man. He was clean-shaven and had straight white teeth. He was wearing a plaid wool shirt and clean jeans. Knowing he had touched me to take off my rain gear, I felt embarrassed, then aroused. While I had always been attracted to hermits, I attributed my state of mind to my concussion and perhaps a bit of dehydration. "Don't let me fall asleep," I said, and he looked at me, quizzical.

I tried to sit up, wooziness circling my head like a marble in a funnel, and turned on my back and closed my eyes until the feeling passed.

"I came to visit my father but lost the trail," I said.

"You're very pretty," he said and walked close.

"Water, please," I begged, and he brought me a chipped mug. He poured water from a stoneware pitcher and I drank my fill.

I felt filled with wanton lust. I took off my glasses and patted the mat and said in a voice as thick as yogurt, "Come here." A moment later and he was lying beside me, his strong arms clinging to my back, his hands finding their way under my waistband and bra.

When I kissed him, I forgot about my father, forgot about my mother, forgot about my research, forgot about everything except his tongue circling my mouth and the warmth and pressure of his groin against my thighs. He tasted like coffee and smelled like pine and smoke and the curious part of sweat. We pulled off clothes and tangled our limbs, the sound of our fast breaths obscuring the pounding rain upon the roof. I shuddered, anxious for him to enter me. We did it; I lost track of the world. I gripped him and held him close until long after we had finished, not ready for him to fall away.

My hermit, I thought. My darling hermit.

He made me ramen noodles for dinner. It was so sweet, how he cared and cooked for me. I'd had several relationships, but none so nurturing. I felt ridiculously rapturously infatuated. I fantasized what it would be like to form an alternative familial grouping with him.

I learned his name: Kirby. I learned that he had lived in this cabin for five years, that long ago he had been married for a year and now had an adult daughter he had not seen since infancy. This made me sad but he swore she was better off without him, which got me to worrying that maybe he wasn't such a nice guy as he seemed. I tried to be analytical, and decided that Kirby was honestly describing his inability to nurture others, rather than hinting at a cryptic malicious side.

My father went by the name of Chicago Lansing. His given name was Charles, but he had taken the name "Chicago" as a way of reconnecting with his father, whose last known address was in Illinois. I asked Kirby if he knew of my father, and Kirby nodded and promised to lead me to him the next morning. He hugged and told me he was glad I'd gotten lost and detoured to find him. I drank more water and started to feel almost normal. We made love again, but this time, I'd recovered enough to focus on the fact that we were not using protection. I pictured myself pregnant with Kirby's child. I pictured a shotgun wedding, instigated by my father, of course. The idea of my father attending my wedding pleased me immensely. I thought about what it would be like to mother a child. I called up scenes of children reaching up to kiss their mothers, of children being calmed by a mother's touch.

When I kissed Kirby's forehead, he turned away. My hermit was fully functioning when it came to sex, but was he capable of enduring love? Would he follow the typical hermit pattern and leave us once the baby was born? From a sociological standpoint, I predicted the answer.

I was a carrier, with one affected X and one normal X chromosome (hH). Statistically, there was only a one in four chance of bearing offspring who neither carried nor exhibited the trait. Which would mean that three out of four children wouldn't be capable of bonding with their mother, i.e. me. I sensed that my affair with Kirby was doomed, for a number of reasons, and resigned myself to trying to endure the physicality of a one-night stand in exchange for being taken to my father's in the morning.

We made love again once more that night, mostly he made love, while I counted up the days since my last period and realized with relief that I had a week before ovulation.

"Do you like that?" he asked as he pushed against me, but I was too distracted by counting up all the men I'd ever been intimate with and didn't answer. There were seven of them, every one of them a hermit. It occurred to me that this was a patterned behavior on my part that I had somehow managed to ignore. Being attracted to hermits was certainly related to my being a carrier. I couldn't wait to test the thesis. I felt elated by my discovery. The moment he was finished, I pushed him off and got up to jot down my notes.

Looking back, I should have predicated that my unscheduled meeting with my father would be tense. His need for a highly structured life did not permit spontaneity. When he heard us coming, he barricaded himself in his cabin and threatened me with his shotgun. Kirby took off at the first sign of trouble. "Don't shoot," I'd screamed, "I'm leaving. I shouted that I was leaving a cake two hundred feet from his front door, and that my mother was in the hospital. I wouldn't know until the following year if he had heard either message.

After our next departmental meeting, Brittany Lake took me aside to point out that Rickman had been withdrawn and had made poor excuses for his failure to produce the results of his committee assignments.

"And that's not all," she said. "He canceled his graduate seminars this week and last and was a half an hour late for his freshman survey class!"

My mother was in rehab, recovering slowly and unable to prevent me from visiting. I felt stressed and under pressure. I did not like assuming an authoritative role, yet that was my job as head of the department. I called and left a message asking Rickman to schedule a meeting, ASAP. He did not return my call, nor the ones after that.

Feeling rash, perhaps because of all I had been through, I drove to Rickman's house and pounded on the door. When he let me in, I saw he had been drinking, and noted that his personal appearance was inconsistent with his usual punctilious standards. He led me to the living room and I took a seat on the couch. "When was the last time you shaved?" I asked.

He wiped his mouth on his sleeve and said, "Why are you here?"

"I'm concerned about your performance," I said, but that sounded too impersonal, given the circumstances. "What's going on?"

He refilled his glass and offered me a shot of whiskey.

I declined, yet he pressed the glass into my hands. He sat next to me.

"Salud," he said, and downed his whiskey.

I took a drink to be polite.

"What in the world is wrong with you?" I asked. "You need to stop drinking and get yourself together."

He shook his head. "You don't know what it's like," he said. "You don't know what it's like to love and lose." He poured another shot. "She's gone," he said. "My wife. She left me."

"I'm sorry," I said. So this boiled down to a typical domestic dispute. Somehow, Rickman hadn't seemed the type to fall into such mundane matters.

Rickman had neglected his wife and she'd run off with another man, a graduate student actually. I knew that having a graduate student steal your wife was thought to be the ultimate emasculation of an academic, worse than the failure to achieve tenure or win grants and awards, but it was a guy thing and I didn't really care. I tried to fake sympathy.

Suddenly, Rickman lurched forward and grabbed at my breasts. He held them in his hands like he was squeezing old grapefruits for juice. His tongue slobbered over my neck.

Disgusted, I gave him a gentle push him away, but he was like sand leaking from a sandbag and was all over me.

"You're so beautiful," he said, passing his wet lips over my cheeks.

Now where had I heard that before? I felt his erection brush my thigh and was about to knee him in the nads when I experienced a vivid flashback that returned me to my last brief touch with rapture. Not to the pleasure part, but to the biological imperative. I thought about my limited social interactions and the likelihood of future pairings.

Rickman was not my type (hermit), but here he was, drunk and offering to mate. All I had to do was lie there; Rickman could do the rest. He was not an unattractive man, plus, he would be able to provide child support. It was also possible that he'd want some part in parenting, though that seemed too much to hope for.

Rickman was an—XY kind of guy. Any products of conception between the two of us would have only a one in four chance of developing full-blown Hikikomori, and only a one out of four chance of being a carrier. Looking on the bright side, there were two out of four chances the baby would be completely normal, and three out of four chances the baby would be capable of loving me.

The odds looked pretty good.

The unhappy cycle could end with me. Looking at the men I'd been intimate with, looking back through my own family history, looking rationally at all I knew about alternative family groupings, clearly it was Rickman or bust.

"Are your parents still living?" I asked.

"Yes," he said, sounding even sadder. "All they wanted was for me to be happy, to give them grandchildren."

My excitement at hearing this made my heart beat faster. I patted Rickman's back and made soothing there, there noises as I figured out exactly where I was in my cycle. The timing was right. My pleasure was increased, knowing that I was using a sociological approach to manipulate nature.

"Pour me another drink," I said, and took off my glasses.

Leslie What is a Nebula Award-winning writer and the author of a novel, *Olympic Games,* and a short story collection, *The Sweet and Sour Tongue.* She has worked as a charge nurse in a nursing home, in an unlocked psychiatric facility, as a manager for a low-income meal site, and as a maskmaker and artist. She currently teaches in The Writers' Program at UCLA Extension. Her work has been published in a number of anthologies and journals, including *Parabola, Asimov's, The MacGuffin, Realms of Fantasy, The Clackamas Review, SciFiction,* and *Midstream.* Called "The Queen of Gonzo" by Gardner Dozois, her work has been been translated into German, Italian, French, Japanese, Russian, Greek, and Klingon.

For other Wordcraft of Oregon titles,
please visit our website
at <u>www.wordcraftoforegon.com</u>

Breinigsville, PA USA
18 August 2009
222540BV00001B/78/P